The Maltese Parrot

A Patricia Fisher Mystery

Book 9

Steve Higgs

Text Copyright © 2019 Steven J Higgs

Publisher: Steve Higgs

The right of Steve Higgs to be identified as author of the Work has been asserted by him in accordance with the Copyright, Designs and Patents Act 1988

All rights reserved.

The book is copyright material and must not be copied, reproduced, transferred, distributed, leased, licensed or publicly performed or used in any way except as specifically permitted in writing by the publishers, as allowed under the terms and conditions under which it was purchased or as strictly permitted by applicable copyright law. Any unauthorised distribution or use of this text may be a direct infringement of the author's and publisher's rights and those responsible may be liable in law accordingly.

'The Maltese Parrot' is a work of fiction. Names, characters, businesses, organisations, places, events and incidents either are the product of the author's imagination or are used fictitiously. Any resemblance to actual persons, living or dead, events or locations is entirely coincidental.

Dedication

For my sister, Karen, who insists on buying every single one of my books in paperback and now has a shelf filled with them.

Sorry, sis, there's a lot more books to come.

Table of Contents:

Valetta

Club Rhumbla

Secret Contact

What Next?

Local Police

Interview

Taxi Driver

The Conversation

A Night of Passion

A Very British Spy

Wanted

Catacombs

The Team

Mrs Garland

Malta Royal Navy Base

Valetta Market

Help Needed

The Snatch

The Lure

The Trap

The Unexpected Element

The Maltese Parrot

Stupid Mass Storage Device

Author note:

Valetta

I looked at the tiny data storage device in my right hand. Last night, or more accurately, in the early hours of this morning, I stumbled exhausted into my bedroom to find a man waiting for me. He was in a chair and fully dressed rather than naked and in my bed thankfully, but he had a gun fitted with a silencer and he had my full attention.

The man claimed to be British Intelligence and in need of my help. So, here I was with a data storage device he claimed to contain the details of a new super-weapon, and tasked with getting it to his contact because he was being chased by the Chinese spies he stole it from.

I sighed and put it in my handbag.

Outside my windows, the city of Valetta in Malta loomed large. Built on a natural escarpment of rock, it had high walls to keep ancient marauders at bay and had withstood the ravages of time for centuries. I was very much looking forward to exploring it.

My name is Patricia Fisher. I like to think of myself as an ordinary, middle-aged woman, though I am beginning to wonder if I am fooling myself about the ordinary bit because no one else seems to see me that way.

Not anymore.

A short while ago, I had a boring life and an unfulfilling marriage and never once thought to question either. All that changed when I caught my husband in bed with my BFF. Fleeing from the situation, and with my decision-making process fuelled by gin, I boarded a cruise liner using all the money in my husband's bank accounts and left that life behind.

In the last couple of months, a lot has changed. I have a new boyfriend, I have a butler, I am semi-famous though I really do not like the attention, but all those things are trivial. What has really changed is me. I stopped trudging through my life and began questioning what I wanted to get out of it. I began challenging myself and because in doing so I created a hurdle to overcome, I discovered a sense of achievement when I did. So, next time, I set the bar higher. It sort of backfired because now I have to wear dark glasses and a hat whenever I leave my suite because otherwise people recognise me. It doesn't help that I am on a cruise ship where the small population ensures word travels fast.

'Your bags are packed, madam,' announced Jermaine as I joined him in the suite's living area.

'Thank you, Jermaine.' Jermaine is my butler, a tall Jamaican man with a fake English accent he learned from watching Downton Abbey. He is mine simply because the only cabin available to me, when I turned up at the port with my bags packed and no ticket, was the Royal Suite. Designed for when the ship carries members of a royal household, it is palatial inside and bigger than the detached country house I lived in with my husband.

I couldn't afford it.

However, a little bit of lady luck, a twist of fate, and the fickle finger of fortune made my first few days on board the ship rather more interesting than expected: I stumbled over a dead body, somehow solved a thirty-year-old mystery, and ended up with the suite for free throughout my three-month around the world cruise.

That was all coming to an end soon. There were just a handful of stops left before the Aurelia, the world's largest and finest cruise ship, arrived back in Southampton where I would have to depart. The thought brought me sadness, but I also felt ready to face reality again. I had to get a divorce and find a place to live plus find a job because I had no income. Cleaning other people's houses - what I did before the cruise - no longer appealed. Not that it ever had. I couldn't see me going back to it now though.

'Are you ready, madam?' asked Jermaine. A porter, presumably summoned by Jermaine to take my bags down, waited in the lobby of my suite, unable to enter the suite proper until my butler gave him permission.

'Yes, Jermaine. Thank you.' I was dating the captain of the ship, Alistair Huntley. He was a year older than me, had never been married and was dangerously handsome. His position as captain and the demands of the role made our rendezvous difficult, but not so difficult as my proclivity for getting into trouble. In the last few weeks, I had been shot at, attacked by an axe-wielding homicidal maniac, threatened by gangsters, held prisoner on numerous occasions and found myself naked or semi-naked in public so regularly it was shocking.

The Aurelia was docked in Valetta for two nights, the captain and I electing to book ourselves into a plush hotel where the likelihood of disturbance was minimal. So I found it ironic that I was now charged with the task of finding the British spy's contact so I could deliver the super-weapon plans. I wanted to ignore it, but he told me the security of the world and the lives of millions depended on me and that my country would owe me a great debt of gratitude.

How was I supposed to say no to that?

The porter had a trolley for my bags, three times what I would need because Jermaine packed for me. I would have thrown in some clean knickers, my toothbrush, and maybe a change of clothes, but he spent hours pressing and neatly folding everything in my wardrobe to ensure I had a selection for any event from afternoon tea to swimming in a lake. It was just after noon, my stomach reminding me that I should eat as I made my way down to the royal suites' exit. That we got our own exit and didn't have to leave with the riffraff should give you an indication of just how much the suites cost.

My bags would find their way to the hotel; all part of the royal suites' service, and Alistair would join me in a couple of hours once the ship was secure and his tasks complete. In the meantime, I was meeting a friend for lunch.

Lady Mary Bostihill-Swank was what the English would call posh totty. Born into money, she grew up being educated to a high level in Swiss schools yet never had to work a day in her life. She inherited a wildlife park located not far from where I grew up, so through the mutual link of geography, we had formed a friendship. Then some gangsters tried to kill us both and our bond strengthened through the mutual use of gin to calm our nerves.

She was married to a well-known author who was currently away on a book tour promoting his latest murder mystery. At a loose end, and with no concern for trivial things like money, she booked herself a suite on the ship for the final ten days return voyage to Southampton. Apparently, when you have so much money that you don't even know how much money you have, just booking a suite for a cruise was a thing you could do.

Leaving Jermaine to sort out my luggage, I clipped my little Dachshund, Anna, onto her lead and left the suite. Lady Mary had texted me last night to say she decided on an earlier flight and got to Valetta in time for dinner last night. She was waiting for me on the quayside now.

From the royal suites on the top deck to the private exit on deck seven took less than five minutes, the journey mostly conducted in an elevator. From the elevator, the exit was no distance at all, so I emerged into the sunlight excited to see my friend again and paused at the top of the gangplank to look for her.

With the additional height my raised position gave me, she was easy to spot, dressed not unlike me in a summer dress with a wide-brimmed sun hat and sunglasses. She was a few years my senior and a dress size smaller, the tiny waistline maintained by drinking most of her meals from a highball glass.

I waved to her and she waved to me and I made my way down the gangplank, Anna pulling me all the way in her keenness to explore. There were thousands of passengers milling about on the quayside, all pouring out of the ship and either getting into taxis or electing to walk into the ancient walled city. There were waiting Purple Star Cruise Lines owned limousines at my disposal if I wanted one; all part of the royal suites treatment, but Valetta wasn't a big place and the walk to it from the purpose-built cruise ship dock just far enough to be worthwhile.

Lady Mary opened her arms in greeting as I drew near. 'Patricia, darling. So wonderful to see you again. How are you? You look so well.'

I hugged her in return, glad to have an unattached woman my own age to speak with. 'I feel good, Mary. Life is treating me well. I need to introduce you to someone I picked up along the way.' Little Anna was already pawing at Lady Mary's legs. Starved of attention, she felt a desperate need to draw the new person's focus down to her level. I scooped her into the air. 'This is Anna.'

'It's a dog,' Lady Mary correctly identified.

'A miniature Dachshund.'

'Wherever did you find a dog on a cruise ship? She looks pregnant too.'

I couldn't fault her powers of observation so as we turned toward Valetta, half a mile ahead of us, I began to tell her about Tokyo and the crazy adventure I had there. However, we didn't get far because raised voices drew our attention. They drew my attention especially because they were shouting my name.

'Patricia Fisher!' I couldn't see who was shouting but it was more than one voice. That time it had been a woman calling for me.

'Patricia Fisher!' This time a man, his voice strong and clear and with an English accent.

With our heads turned toward the commotion they were making, we could see someone barging through the crowd of passengers heading to the city. They were coming against the tide, pushing and shoving and generally upsetting people if the number of curse words were anything to go by.

I glanced at the ship. Could I make it back inside and get to safety before they found me? I didn't think so. They must have spotted me when I came onto the raised gangplank. And though they surely couldn't see me now, they were making a beeline for me and there was no way I could avoid them.

They burst through the straggling back end of the crowd, a man and a woman, with two teenage kids in tow. They looked to me like typical Brits on holiday; a bit sunburnt from their desperate attempt to get a tan to show off at work upon their return home, milky white skin where the sun hadn't yet had a chance to do its damage, and nothing but trashy designer labels even though they wore sports kit that had most likely never seen the inside of a gym. I told myself off for being judgemental, accepted that I was trapped, and greeted them with a smile.

'Can I help you?' I asked.

'Can you help us?' echoed the woman. Anna dived forward to repel them as they got within striking range. They came directly for me and she didn't like that at all. Or maybe she just didn't like the look of them. I had managed to train her out of biting people. More or less. But I think she might have challenged the policy for the family now crowding us.

The woman danced back to avoid Anna's lunge, the Dachshund attack stopping her from saying whatever it was she had to say. I reeled Anna in and picked her up, scratching under her ears to sooth her.

'Can she help us?' repeated the man.

'Hey, it's Granny Pants!' cheered the teenage boy, a rather round child of about fourteen with a phone permanently attached to his pudgy right hand.

'Excuse me?' I asked, my eyebrows knitting into one as I scowled at him.

His mother slapped him around the back of the head, knocking a few swearwords loose in the process. 'I told you not to call her that, Gary' she spat at him.

'And don't talk to your mother like that,' the father insisted, berating the boy for the cursing he undoubtedly learned from his parents.

'Tell her not to hit me then,' whined Gary, rubbing the back of his head and drifting away, his focus solely on his phone.

'Sorry,' the woman apologised. 'You do your best...' I didn't have children, but I had to believe that most parents achieved a best way above the level she aimed for. I kept quiet since my first question was yet to be answered. 'Sorry,' she said again. 'It's my mother, you see.'

I waited for there to be more, so when there wasn't any, I said, 'No, I'm afraid I don't follow. What about your mother?'

The man spoke, 'She's been taken.'

'We don't know that,' protested the woman.

I hadn't had an answer to my first question, but the conversation was moving on and getting confusing. 'You say someone's been taken?' I asked.

'Yes,' the woman replied, now sounding exasperated. 'My mother has been taken.'

Her husband talked over her before she could say anything else, 'She's been grabbed by sex traffickers. She was with us one minute and gone the next. To them, she's a woman travelling alone. I told you we needed to keep her on a leash,' he complained to his wife.

I closed my eyes and opened them again, shaking my head as I did. 'I'm sorry. I still don't follow. How is it that you think I can help you?'

The woman glanced at her husband and then back at me, a look of confusion now ruling her face. 'Well, you're the super sleuth, that's what people keep saying. We saw you on the news: The Saviour of Zangrabar. Wherever there's mystery, Patricia Fisher will solve it. That's you, isn't it?'

I was still struggling a little to understand why I was involved in this conversation, but it was beginning to feel painfully obvious what they expected of me. 'You think I can help find your mother?'

'That's what you do, isn't it?' asked the woman, clearly perplexed. 'People show you a mystery and then you find the bad guys behind it.'

'No, not really,' I relied wearily. 'I just happened to trip over a couple of cases and work out the answers.' Okay, it sounded a little weak when I said it like that, and it wasn't really true either. During the last couple of months I had learned that I was really quite tenacious, and possessed a mind which could unravel clues to find the truth hidden beneath them. 'What makes you think she was taken?' I asked.

'Taken by sex traffickers,' the man corrected me.

'We don't know that,' the woman argued again.

He turned to his wife as if frustrated by her. 'We saw her in the back of a taxi. They grabbed her and drove off. What could it be, if it's not sex traffickers?'

My brain wanted to shout that it could be lots of things. To get away from her family would be top of the list of probable reasons, though I elected to keep that thought quiet. 'Couldn't it be that she decided to explore on her own?' I asked.

The man actually laughed. 'Her mum? You've got to be kidding. She don't do anything or go anywhere if she can help it. We had to more or less force her to come on this holiday.'

'I bet you did,' mumbled Lady Mary under her breath.

The woman agreed with her husband. 'He's right. Mum doesn't like to go out much. She would never set off on her own. We were one of the first off the ship, keen to explore, so we were looking around in the shops and talking about getting some food and suddenly she wasn't with us. Then Gary spotted her in the back of a taxi. We shouted for her but there was a man on the backseat with her and it was clear he was holding her in place.' A tear leaked down her face which made me feel bad because all I wanted to do was get away from them.

I couldn't shift the feeling that I ought to be getting paid for this sort of thing if I was going to do it. I filed the thought away for later consideration.

Lady Mary took off her sunglasses, looked at the woman and pointed to her husband. 'You just called him Gary?'

'Yes. That's his name.'

'And your boy's name is…'

'Gary,' the woman supplied.

'Right. Jolly good. Just checking.' Lady Mary put her sunglasses back on but risked a glance in my direction so she could pull a face.

I glanced between her and the tearful woman with her tubby husband and let my shoulders slump; I was going to try to help them, I just couldn't see a way of saying no. 'Okay, okay.' I hauled a notebook and a pen from my bag. 'I need a couple of details first.' I took the name of the missing grandmother which was Nora Garland. Her daughter was Sarah Tanner, both the boys were called Gary and her skinny daughter's name was Chardonnay. Then I asked where they were when they last saw Nora. I kept checking my watch because I had only a limited amount of time do whatever I was going to do with them and get to my rendezvous with Justin's contact in Club Rhumbla on Old Mint Street.

I wasn't sure what they expected of me. So far as I could make out, the woman's mother had chosen to give herself some peace for a day, taking off by herself for once. So I was going through the motions and putting them into one of the Purple Star Lines private limousines so it could take us to the location they last saw her.

'Cor, this motor is wicked,' said young Gary with a reverent tone as we climbed inside the elegant car.

'Don't touch anything,' instructed his father, just as his son was helping himself to a decanter of brandy. It was swiftly snatched from his grasp and put back into the bar.

'Where can I take you, Mrs Fisher,' asked the driver, turning slightly in the front seat to make eye contact, the leather squeaking as he did.

In turn, I made eye contact with Sarah. 'Where do we need to go?' I asked, prompting her to give the driver the location she last saw her mother.

'Oh, um, have you got a map?' she asked. 'I don't know the name of the road. It was just along from something called the Malta experience.'

In the front, the driver fiddled with something made of paper, the tell-tale crinkling sound suggesting he was folding something to open it out. Then he held up a map, folded to reveal the piece she referred to. 'Quarry Wharf?' he asked. 'Down by the water?'

Sarah peered at it. 'Yes, that looks about right.'

We set off in silence, six of us squeezed into the rear of the large car with both parents constantly telling their kids to stop messing with its contents. Mercifully, Malta is a small place and the ancient walled city of Valetta is even smaller, so we were only in the car for a few minutes. It didn't pass quietly though. Sarah Tanner struck up a conversation as soon as the car set off. 'Thank you so much for helping us. My mum must be so scared right now. I don't know what I would do if anything happened to her.'

'Sell her big house and book another cruise,' Gary Junior laughed, ducking the next slap as it swung at the back of his head.

Now that he had drawn attention to himself, I had a question. 'What is Granny Pants?' The teenage boy chortled, which elicited a further slap to the back of his head, this one landing before he could duck.

'We need this lady's help, Gary,' his mother growled at him. He swore again, which made me feel like giving him a slap myself.

'Show her,' insisted the boy's father.

'Show me what?' I asked, not entirely sure I wanted to see.

The boy clearly didn't like being given orders, but the father snatched the phone from his hands, fended off the child trying to take it back and pulled up what he wanted to show me. 'You're famous,' sneered the boy as the screen was offered.

There, on a website called *Granny Pants* was my bum. Upside down where I fell off the stage in Zangrabar, a camera managed to catch me with my legs folded over my head to show the world my hold-everything-in knickers. I was the website's granny of the month; their star pin up if you like. The internet equivalent of a centrefold.

I was mortified. All the little brat could do was grin. Almost three months at sea, a lifetime's worth of adventures and it was just like the first day when my luggage spilled open as I tried to get to the ship.

I handed the phone back to Gary the father, hoping he would make Gary the brat eat it. The rest of the journey was conducted in silence, no one daring to say a word. Four or maybe five minutes later, the limousine glided to a stop and the driver announced we had arrived. I thanked him as we all got out and let him go. When we were done here, we could walk to wherever was next. It was a beautiful day in Valetta; the sun beat down from high in the sky with barely a cloud to be seen but I was failing to appreciate it because I had let myself get caught up in whatever new mystery this was.

Pointing to the shop right in front of us, Sarah said, 'We were right here. Then I noticed mum wasn't with us and turned around to look for her. I thought she might still be in the last shop.'

Gary took over the story. 'That's when I saw her in the back of the taxi. It swept by us, but I managed to get a picture.' He held up his phone, but the picture was little more than a blur, no way of using it to identify the people inside. The only thing I could see was the arm of a crazy, garish, red and blue stripy shirt on the person in the back.

'Is that your mother?' I asked.

Sarah and Gary both leaned in to see what I pointed to. 'No,' gasped Sarah. 'Who's that with her? Gary, there's someone in the taxi with her. That's who took her!'

'Did you take any other shots?' I asked. 'One with the licence plate or the name of the taxi firm on?'

'Goodness, I hadn't thought of that.' Gary shook his head, berating himself for not thinking the way that I did.

'I told you she was good,' Sarah bragged.

I peered around his arm as he scrolled through the phone. 'Oh, wow,' he exclaimed in surprise. 'Look, I have the licence plate and the number for the taxi firm.' Using my phone, I dialled the number. This was going to be easy.

While I waited for the phone to connect, I said, 'Can you send me that picture?' I might not need it, but I might have to send it to the taxi firm to help me identify the cab. Or the man, perhaps.

'Valetta Taxis, good afternoon.' The voice at the other end was that of a middle-aged woman who smoked too many cigarettes; a rasping croak rather more than a voice.

'Hello, my friend got into one of your cabs just a short while ago. It picked her up from Quarry Wharf at about...' I motioned for Gary to fill in the blank.

'Oh,' he said, suddenly realizing what I wanted, 'about twelve o'clock.'

'About twelve o'clock,' I repeated. 'We have managed to lose contact and she isn't answering her phone. Can you tell me where it dropped off if I give you the licence plate?'

'Sure. There should be a two-digit number on the cab though. That will be faster.'

I checked the picture again; Gary still had the screen toward me so I could see. 'Twenty-seven?' I tried, assuming but not certain I had the number she referred to.

In the background, she had a brief conversation with someone in Maltese, keeping me waiting for more than a minute before she came back on the line. 'That taxi went to Sliema. Dropped off on Sur Fons Street near Balluta Bay. If you want to go there, I can have a driver with you in about a minute.'

'Can you just give me a moment, please?' I pulled the phone away from my ear. 'Your mother went to Sliema. The taxi firm can send a car to take to you to the same place they dropped her off if you wish.'

'Sliema? Where the heck's Sliema?' asked Gary.

'It's the next town along, Dad,' said Gary Junior without looking up from his phone.

Gary Senior screwed his face up. 'How the heck do you know that, Gary?'

'Google Maps, Dad,' he replied, still showing no sign of ever taking his eyes off the phone in his hands.

Prompting a response, I said, 'You can have a car here almost immediately, but I need to give the lady an answer now. Shall I say yes?'

'Of course, yes,' said Sarah in frustration when Gary failed to answer immediately.

I relayed the answer and put my phone away.

'Oh, thank you, thank you, thank you,' Sarah gushed. 'I knew you would sort this out for us. I can't imagine what we would have ever done without you.'

'Hold on,' said Gary Senior, before I could tell her it was nothing. 'We haven't found her yet. If the sex traffickers have got her, all we'll find in Sliema is a dead end and a taxi bill. What's the good of going to Sliema if the sex traffickers have got her?'

Sarah joined her husband in staring at me for an answer. I was getting a bit miffed now. I helped them because they were too dumb to think their own way out of the problem, and now they expected me to do… what? Chase around the island until they found her having coffee somewhere quietly and enjoying her brief bout of peace? Not a chance. 'I'm sure she won't have been taken by sex traffickers…'

'How do you know that?' demanded Gary. 'If she hasn't been snatched by someone, why isn't she answering her phone?' I had an answer for that, but I didn't think this was the time to air my views on their family.

I was trying to listen to what he was saying, but behind Gary, we had caught the attention of a pair of men in business suits. They were African, I thought, Algerian maybe, which I believed bordered the sea on the North African coast. Geography had never been a good subject at school and school was a long way behind me now. They had emerged from the shadows of some shops that bordered the streets, or at least that was what I thought at first, but now I saw it was an alleyway between the shops.

They were having a conversation and seemed to be discussing us.

'Are you listening?' prompted Gary, snapping my attention back.

I tried to focus on him but one of the men was pointing at me and the other was playing with his phone, constantly casting his eyes down at it and then back up at me. 'I'm sorry, you were saying?' I asked.

Gary gave an I-give-up flap of his arms. 'What do we do if we get there and there's no sign of her?' he asked, clearly repeating himself and unhappy about having to do so.

'I would suggest you call the police, Mr Tanner. Doesn't that sound like a good idea? The local police will have local knowledge and be able to coordinate a response if, indeed, your mother-in-law does prove hard to find.'

'That's your advice?' asked Sarah, her expression almost a sneer. 'My mother's been taken by sex traffickers and you want us to call the local police. Are we keeping you from your lunch or something?' The Tanners were about as unpleasant as you could get, I decided. They didn't deserve my help, most especially because I was convinced the absent Mrs Garland had simply slipped away from them for the sake of her own sanity.

I bit down my response though, reminding myself that I was British and rudeness on their part need not force me to lower my standards. 'I wish you luck in finding your mother, Mrs Tanner,' I replied with as much conviction as I could manage. 'I am sure she will prove to be fine and is not answering her phone because she has accidentally knocked it onto silent.'

'And if we don't find her, we should call the police,' echoed Gary. 'Fat lot of use you were. Some detective.' He turned away so he could mutter obscenities under his breath and set a great example for his children to follow.

I had been dismissed. Keeping my head up and my rage inside, I let Anna tug me along. Beside me, Lady Mary kept quiet, wise enough to let me stew by myself for a while. Once I left the awful family behind and allowed my pace to slow, she said, 'I dare say it is gin o'clock, sweetie. Shall we avail ourselves of the first establishment and see what passes for a cocktail here?'

I couldn't help but smile, she was just incorrigible, but a gin sounded good. I figured I had just enough time, so I pushed thoughts of the missing granny and her awful family from my mind and looked up at the giant walls of Valetta looming large above us. I had missed most of Greece because of misadventure there, so I wasn't going to miss Malta too.

Had I not been so absorbed by committing the architecture, sights and smells to memory, I might have had time to glance about and notice the Algerian gentlemen still watching me.

Club Rhumbla

One gin and tonic quickly became two, plus a snack, or a snackcident as Barbie liked to call them. Any food that fell outside of one's planned calorie intake for the day was a snackcident, which, in her world, was a very bad thing. I got that it was counterintuitive to my work in the gym and general focus on being healthy and fit, but… well, let's see how focused Barbie is at fifty-three.

Laughing with Lady Mary as I retold the story of the escape from the harem in Zangrabar and the dirty old British ambassador who kept trying to get in my knickers, I glanced at the clock behind the bar and said a rude word.

'Whatever is it, sweetie?' asked Lady Mary.

'I have to be somewhere.'

'Goodness, where? You just arrived.' I was out of my chair, but Lady Mary hadn't moved yet.

I paused, trying to decide what to tell her. It was safer if she knew nothing about the spy stuff and the secret weapon. My meeting with the contact would take seconds and, once over, I could continue my day with no further concerns. 'I have to meet someone, and I only have twelve minutes to find the place and get to him. I won't be long; you might as well wait here.'

Lady Mary sprang to her feet. 'Stuff that, darling. This is the most excitement I have had since that business with the gangsters.' I was almost running when I left the bar, Lady Mary hot on my heels as I tried to orientate myself to the map in my head. 'Where are we going, sweetie?' she called after me.

'I can't tell you,' I shouted back.

'Ooh, mysterious. I like it. What are you going there for?'

'I can't tell you that either.' The voice in my head said it was for her own good that she know as little as possible. However, I wasn't surprised when I got a snippy reply.

'That's not much to go on, Patricia. I want some adventure. Why do you think I came back?'

I had no answer for her so I hurried on, pulling Lady Mary along in my slip stream until I spotted the sign sticking out two stories up. I had found the place at least. With only six minutes to spare, I wasted no time. 'Mary, I need to do this alone. I won't be long at all. Can you wait here for me?' We were right next to a bar with tables spilling into the street. Half of the tables were already occupied by tourists and locals getting some lunch.

She gave me a disappointed frown. 'Wait here in this bar, darling? I could just as easily have waited in the bar we were in. Why did I race around here with you if you expect me to hang around and miss all the intrigue and adventure?'

I expected as much and took hold of her hand to impart how serious I was. 'Mary, I don't know if what I am about to do is dangerous or not. It shouldn't be, but it could be that people, dangerous people, are watching.'

'Is that why we are being followed?' she asked.

Her question caught me by surprise. 'Someone is following us?'

'Yes. They were pretty good at it too. I thought I spotted someone when we were in the last place but every time I looked, there was nothing but a shadow where I thought they should be. Then, when we were running to get here, I could hear their footsteps following us as they echoed between the buildings. I haven't seen who it is yet, but someone is back there. Someone with dark skin.'

I remembered the way the two men had been watching me down on Quarry Wharf and a sense of dread crept up my spine to make me feel giddy with fear, which was in direct contrast to Lady Mary who looked giddy with excitement. Were we about to get murdered by international spies? I cursed myself for watching too many James Bond movies, pushed the thought from my mind and focused on the task I promised to perform. I patted her hand again. 'You'll be safe in this bar; there are too many people in it for anyone to try something. I will be back in less than five minutes. All I have to do is drop something off.' She looked unhappy. 'Please?' I begged.

Miffed, she plonked her handbag down on the nearest table and waved for the waiter. 'Alright, Patricia.' I could tell she wasn't happy from her snippy tone. 'This is not the level of excitement I expected though.'

'I'm leaving Anna with you,' I ventured, tying Anna's lead to Lady Mary's chair without waiting for her to agree. As she folded herself demurely into a chair and gave me a cold shoulder, I promised myself I would make it up to her later, before hurrying along the road to the club's entrance.

A pleasant looking, yet broad and tall doorman in his forties smiled as I approached, nodding his head in greeting. So, it came as a surprise when he lifted a hand to waist height to stop me before I could pass him and enter. 'Gentlemen only, madam.'

'You're kidding me.'

His eyebrows lifted in surprise. 'No, madam. This is a private club for men. First established in 1904 by the Royal Navy, it caters to the quiet, dignified tastes of refined gentlemen.' In my head, I translated that to mean it was a seedy strip club, but I still needed to get in.

'I'm meeting someone inside,' I explained. 'I only need to be in there for one minute. No more than that.'

'That doesn't sound like much of a meeting,' he argued.

I blew out a frustrated breath and started again. 'I just need to give something to a person who is waiting inside. Can I do that?'

He shook his head, 'No. But if you give it to me, I will make sure he gets it.'

That wasn't going to happen. 'I can't do that. I... it has to be me. It is quite sensitive.'

Now the man's face clouded. 'Is this about drugs? Are you trying to do a drug drop off in this club?' He loomed over me, making himself look threatening, which wasn't very hard for him, let me assure you.

I took a step back to give myself some space. 'No!' I protested. 'It's nothing like that. It's just sensitive and personal and my friend is in there waiting for me right now.'

He relaxed his posture slightly, still eyeing me suspiciously, 'Well, your friend should have picked a better meeting place. Not even the cleaners here are women.'

I let the misogynistic comment slide, accepted that I wasn't going to make my 1400hrs rendezvous and bid him a good day. Now I had a problem though. National importance; that was what Justin the spy claimed. It was of national importance that I deliver the data on the little black stick thingy, and I had already managed to mess up getting to the contact on time. Now I had to find another way in. And quickly.

I glanced about and crossed the street. Lady Mary still had her back to me so she couldn't see what I was doing. She had a compact out by the look of it, touching up her makeup most likely, and there was no sign of anyone following me, dark-skinned or otherwise, so I put that fanciful tale down to her imagination.

Around the corner I found a tourist shop. It had ornaments and postcards and bric-a-brac items but not what I wanted. I found the items I sought on the third attempt, in a shop selling everything from cigars to hub caps. Precious time ticked by, but with a final check in the mirror, I decided I might pass muster provided the man was blind and chose not to look my way.

I had bought a man's suit. It was second hand, but it just about fit my chest once I also bought bandages and tied my boobs as flat as I could get them. I won't claim it was comfortable, but they were hidden, and I shouldn't need to remain like this for long. I bought men's brogues which were four sizes too big and stuffed the toes with an extra pair of socks. A short-haired brown wig and a battered brown fedora hat did their best to hide my face and blond hair. Then a white shirt and a black tie finished the outfit. I looked more like Sam Spade than Patricia Fisher, which was a good thing, but I also looked like my outfit had just escaped from the 50s.

What I needed now, was to hope some other men were going in so I could tag onto the back of their group.

I shrugged at my reflection one last time in a here-goes-nothing kind of a way. Stuffed my own clothes into a carrier bag and asked the shopkeeper to mind them for a few minutes.

Across the road, the doorman was still at his station, watching passers-by impassively though he always nodded and smiled if he caught anyone's eye. I approached in a casual way, changing my gait halfway across the road as I reminded myself to walk like a man.

How does a man walk, Patricia?

I had no idea what that was supposed to look like. I tried to imagine having testicles hanging in the way then rejected the idea because I would look ridiculous trying to walk with my legs open to let them swing. Instead, I gave my groin a scratch as I saw men do absentmindedly all the time and thought about spitting on the floor. I couldn't bring myself to do that but decided the character I was playing wasn't a teenage boy so wouldn't do that anyway.

The doorman's gaze swung my way as I crossed the street, his eyes lingering for a second before moving on to look at four other men who were hurrying past me. They wore Ralph Lauren polo shirts in bright colours, tan shorts and white sports shoes. Their destination was obvious; they were going right for the club and they looked so different from me that I saw my error – I wasn't going to blend in at all.

The doorman welcomed them with a nod, the four young men in their late twenties all darting up the stairs behind him to get to the nefarious delights beyond. Any second now, he was going to swing his attention back to the street and he would look at me and know I didn't belong. He couldn't miss me; I was heading right for him.

So, I altered my trajectory. I tried to make it look natural but undoubtedly failed miserably. He was probably watching me even as I walked away though I didn't dare check because then he would definitely clock me. Just when I was cursing myself and wondering how on earth I was going to get into the club, serendipity threw me a bone and a side door opened. A man in waiter's garb wrestled his way out through the self-closing door, placing a heavy looking bag of rubbish against the door to prop it open while he carried another across the street to deposit it in a wheelie bin. Before he could make it across the street and turn back, I zipped inside and vanished from sight.

I was in.

Secret Contact

Soft music drifted down the wooden staircase as I climbed it, my feet fast but quiet. It sounded like a someone playing the piano though I didn't question it at the time. I couldn't dawdle for fear I would be caught up to by the man taking out the trash, and I couldn't hurry too much for fear I would run blindly into someone else.

The stairs ended at a fire door. With no way of knowing what was on the other side, I held my breath and shoved it open. Mercifully, it opened into an empty corridor and the increased volume of the piano told me I was very close to the club itself. A toilet flushed, the sound close by, followed by a door opening a few feet ahead of me on the right. A man came out; overweight, balding, and in his fifties, he turned away from me without even noticing I was there, still zipping up his fly as he made his way back to the club. Through double doors on the left as he passed through them, the piano now coming through clearly which told me the club was on the other side.

A gentleman's club. I could think of few things seedier and could never fathom why men wanted to see young women take their clothes off and dance. I imagine it to be thoroughly distracting for them, but in a negative way. Now was not the time for questioning sexual politics though, I steeled myself for what I might see, and pushed the doors open.

I got the shock of my life.

There were no strippers parading their goods on a stage under bright lights. No tacky scenes with lap dancers grinding away above fat businessmen. There were no woman at all, but the men were reading papers, or playing chess. I saw a four in one corner playing bridge. The young men I watched go into the club were nowhere in sight, possibly having also misunderstood the nature of the club and upon discovering its true colours, left as quickly as they had come.

Taking it all in, I remembered what I was there for and thumbed the data storage device in my pocket. Close to the bar, but sitting by himself, and propped against the wall was the contact. He wore a black trilby hat with a feather in it and had a book on the table in front of him. I couldn't see what the book was, but it had to be the right guy. I stole across the room, trying to look casual but couldn't avoid a collision path with a waiter who had just delivered drinks to the table playing bridge.

'Can I bring you a drink, sir?' he asked, pausing before me on his way back to the bar.

I sure was thirsty; my nerves had robbed all the moisture from my mouth. 'Yes,' I said in my normal voice, realised what I had done and coughed as deeply as I could. I tried again, this time doing my best to fake a rumbling bass. 'Yes, thank you. A gin and tonic, please.' I didn't plan to hang around long enough to drink it but not ordering anything might look suspicious.

'Very good, sir.' the waiter replied. 'We have a wide range of gins and of tonics to pair with them. Does sir have a preference?'

I was trying to shake the man off, but he was just doing his job properly. In a bid to get rid of him quickly I said, 'Hendricks over slimline tonic, Fevertree in preference if you have it, and garnished with a slice of cucumber. Lots of ice served in a goblet, not a highball.'

I saw the pleasure on the waiter's face as I ordered it the way he felt it should be served. I got a dip of his head in salute, 'Very good, sir.' Then he left me to fetch the drink and I was finally able to continue onward to my contact.

I was twenty minutes late.

I approached from his side, not creeping up on him, not making my movements overt. I wondered whether I should just sit down but maybe it was more natural to speak to him standing up as if asking to join him. Getting close enough to speak quietly but not whisper, I delivered the code phrase. 'I hope the barman here can make a decent banana daiquiri.'

I waited for his response, but he didn't move. Maybe I spoke too quietly.

I leaned down to get closer to him and tried again. 'I hope the barman here can make a decent banana daiquiri.'

Still no response.

'Patricia, what are you doing?' I screamed when the sudden voice spoke right next to my ear, jumping out of my skin and wheeling around to find Lady Mary standing behind me with Anna in her arms. My dog's tail was wagging away like mad.

'Mary, how did you get in here? It's a gentlemen only club.'

She frowned as if I were being ridiculous. 'The same way women always get into their husband's secret clubs: I bribed the doorman. Why are you dressed like Humphrey Bogart?'

'Your drink, sir,' announced the waiter, offering me a tray with an enticing looking gin and tonic on it.

'I'll have one of those too,' Lady Mary ordered. 'No, wait, better make it two. No, three; Patricia is bound to want another one.'

'Very good, madam,' replied the waiter with another curt nod.

'Would you mind keeping it down, old boy,' asked a gentleman in a tweed suit over the top of his Times newspaper. 'Your wife really ought to wait outside you know, wot?' He had a giant, bristling grey mustache which must have made getting food into his mouth difficult and he reminded me of a retired Brigadier or Admiral. He flapped his paper, disappearing behind it once more, disinterested in whether I had a reply for him or not.

'So, what are you doing here?' Lady Mary asked again, this time her voice a little more quiet.

I let my shoulders slump. 'I'm supposed to be handing something vitally important to this man here but he appears to have fallen asleep.' I poked his shoulder to rouse him. He moved finally, but it was not the kind of movement I hoped for. He pitched forward onto the table, his hat rolling off to reveal an ice pick sticking out of his left ear and a trickle of blood gathering on his collar.

I squealed and jumped back in shock.

Lady Mary said an unladylike word.

Justin's contact, whoever he was, was stone cold dead.

The waiter, who had just been returning with three more gin and tonics, slowed his pace as he saw the man lying on the table, saw the ice pick, and arrived at the wrong conclusion.

Lady Mary and I both watched the colour drain from his face as his feet begin to backpeddle away from us. She lunged forward, swiping the three drinks before he could escape or spill them.

'Help!' he yelled, getting everyone's attention. 'Help, they killed him!'

Lady Mary threw the first gin and tonic into her mouth and lifted the second one, but people were starting to get out of their seats now. On the opposite side of the long oak bar was a pair of rough looking men with five-day stubble. They looked dashing but deadly, their attention focused on me and the dead British Intelligence contact which gave me the instant impression they were in the same game. They weren't Chinese though, they looked more Eastern European to me.

Anna caught sight of them and barked a warning.

Thumping footsteps charging up the stairs at the front of the club drew my attention just before the doorman came into view. Our backs were to a wall and, pincered between the five-day stubble guys and the doorman, there was no way out.

I pulled off my hat and wig, hoping that showing them I was a woman and not a man might help. It surprised a few of the patrons, but no one who was moving in my direction changed their mind.

Lady Mary grabbed my right hand and thrust a drink into it. 'Here. I can't finish them all myself, Patricia; I'm not a machine.' The glass shook in my hand, showing my terror as the men advanced.

The doorman looked royally pissed off. 'So that's why you wanted to get in here so badly? You had to kill someone?'

One of the five-day-stubble men got to us first, dashing across the bar to murmur, 'Give it to me and I will get you out of here. I promise no harm will come to you.' His accent was Serbian maybe. I couldn't hope to pinpoint it better than that, but he knew what I had, and he was asking for it. If it was as important as Justin claimed, then I would be putting lives at risk if I handed it over. My own life couldn't come first. 'Please,' he begged. 'There's no time.'

'May I be of assistance, madam?' asked Jermaine, the sound of his voice so comforting, familiar, and welcome it was like having warm caramel spooned over my brain. It was a rhetorical question, of course, its intent to distract the circle of men pressing in toward me so he could disguise his attack.

Flying feet whipped through the air as he placed his hands on a table and flipped across it to land on top of the five-day stubble guys. They went down but he bounced back up and swung kicks at anyone else that came near. The doorman rushed him, but size and rage were no match for my butler. Lady Mary stepped out of the way and put a hand over her glass to make sure nothing spilled as Jermaine darted forward in a feint, then quickly back again as the doorman committed to his swing. Jermaine caught it, twisted and threw the doorman into the two five-day stubble guys who were just getting up again.

Then my butler/ninja crouched into a defensive posture and slowly scanned around the room, his fists tracking wherever his eyes went. Satisfied no danger remained, he straightened and dusted off his shirt. 'Madam, I feel it might be time to depart.'

'Nearly finished,' said Lady Mary, upending the final glass of gin.

The nervous barman stared open-mouthed. When I returned his gaze, he swallowed and asked, 'How will we be paying today?'

Grabbing Lady Mary's hand, I dragged her from the club before she could order anything else. As we ran for the stairs, the man with the bushy mustache flapped his paper again. 'That's why we don't let women in,' he harrumphed.

What Next?

Outside in the street, I stopped to get my breath but found my arm yanked as Jermaine kept going. Anna had a completely different idea about which way she wanted to go so I was pulled in two different directions and had to fight to make my feet follow Jermaine.

'I need to get my things,' I wailed, trailing along behind him like a kite behind a child. My clothes were still in the shop where I changed.

'No time, madam,' he insisted. For once Jermaine was dressed like a tourist. This was so unusual that, when I thought about it, I could only recall seeing him out of his butler's uniform a handful of times. Twice when he dressed as Steed from the Avengers; fulfilling some personal fantasy for sure, once when he dressed as a stripper to beat up a pair of gangsters and a few times besides when he had cause to. Today he wore loose-fitting tan trousers and a deep green polo shirt.

'What were you doing in that club, Jermaine?' I asked with a deep-rooted suspicion that I would not like his answer. 'I thought you were going to spend the two days here exploring because you have only ever been to Malta once.'

'Yes, madam,' he replied. 'I thought it prudent to keep an eye on you.'

Now I was squinting at him. 'Why, Jermaine? Why did you think it was necessary to check up on me?'

Heading toward a side street as he watched for anyone following, he spared the time to meet my gaze. 'Madam has a habit of finding herself in… situations.' With another glance over his shoulder, he said, 'I really do think we should hurry to get out of sight.'

He was right about the need for haste; the five-day-stubble men appearing in the street a second after we escaped from sight down a side street. I risked a peek back at them, looking through a display of t-shirts hanging outside a shop on the corner.

Both men looked angry about losing me, but neither wasted time blaming the other. We had slipped away and that was how it was. The doorman in his suit exited the door behind them as they started to make their way across the street. They were going away from me, but the doorman had more men spilling out behind him now, the barman who served me gin among those pressed into service. They had a body in their club and a need to find the crazy woman they believed had killed him.

I ducked back around the corner out of sight, trying to decide which way to go now and what to do. I still had the stupid data drive in my pocket. I had to hand it over but had no one to give it to. What was my plan B?

'Are you hurt, madam?' I wanted to be mad at Jermaine. He felt it necessary to follow me and keep me safe so it was him that Lady Mary had spotted in the shadows, not the Algerian men after all. I didn't feel I could berate him for his concern because he had just saved me from the hoodlums in the club. I chose instead to pat his arm in thanks.

'No, Jermaine. I am quite alright.'

He had come to rest with his hands held loosely behind his back; his standard butler's pose. 'Can I ask what you were doing in that gentleman's club, madam? If I am able to assist in whatever you are doing, I will do so gladly.'

'Ooh, yes. I want to know as well, sweetie,' said Lady Mary. 'Dressing up, sneaking into clubs. It's all getting very exciting already.'

Anna pawed my leg, so I picked her up. Her middle was getting bulky already, but I tucked her under my arm where I knew she felt supported and safe as I addressed my friends and tried to work out what to tell them. 'Hold on,' I said as a thought occurred to me. 'How did you know I had gone into the club, Mary. I left you at the restaurant with your back to me.'

To answer my question, she turned around and pulled her compact out. Then pretended to powder her face while looking over her shoulder at me in the mirror. 'One picks up little tricks along the way, dear.' Nodding at her deceptively simple trick, I wondered again about the doorman and the five-day-stubble guys, taking another quick peek around the goods hanging outside the shop. Lady Mary picked up on what I was doing. 'The two rough-looking men in the club, they asked you to give them something. What have you got that they want, Patricia?'

'I can't tell you,' I replied unhappily.

'We can't help you with it if you won't tell us what it is, dear,' she chided in return.

Hanging about where they might spot us wasn't doing us any favours, plus there was a dead body across the street which was going to attract the authorities very soon. 'We should move on,' I suggested. Lady Mary pursed her lips in annoyance; she wanted to know my secret and wanted to get involved. Of course, she didn't know that the information I protected her from might make her a target. 'The police must be on their way,' I pointed out. 'They will be looking for a woman in a man's suit. I need to get my things and get changed before someone spots me or hands out a description.'

The wail of a police siren accentuated my point nicely.

'Yes, okay,' she conceded. 'But soon you will have to tell me what is going on, Patricia. I shall get quite snippy if you don't.' As she drifted further along the side street to where Jermaine waited a few feet away, I shot one last quick look up the street.

'Mrs Fisher,' said the storekeeper as he checked the t-shirts and arranged them for passers-by to see. I was startled by how close he was and that he addressed me by name but when I looked, I saw a man I recognised. It was Justin Metcalf-Howe the British spy, only his tidy brown hair was now covered by a scraggly blonde wig and he had wire-rimmed glasses on. 'Were you able to successfully deliver the item?' he asked. I took a step back. Anna was trying to sniff his leg, pulling against her lead as I tugged her away. 'Kudos on the outfit, by the way. I had no doubt you would find a way to successfully enter the club.'

I shook my head in confusion. 'I wasn't able to deliver the item. Your contact was there but he was dead.'

He processed the information without a single flicker of emotion passing over his face. 'I feared as much. The net is closing faster than I thought.'

'Who are those two?' I jerked my head in the direction of the club. The two stubbly men were still in sight, moving away but scanning the area as they did.

'That's Bogdan and Yuri, a pair of Ukrainian hitmen. They were in the club?'

'They were. Look, I think maybe you should take the... item,' I used the same word he employed, 'back. This is way above my pay grade.'

'Goodness no, Mrs Fisher. You are the perfect person for the task. Keep hold of it and await instructions.'

Lady Mary and Jermaine saw that I hadn't moved and was now talking to someone. They came to join me. 'Hello,' said Lady Mary, addressing the fake shop keeper. 'We don't want to buy anything thank you. Patricia, you said you wanted to move on.'

I turned to look at her and then back to argue with Justin, but he was gone. Bewildered, I lifted the t-shirts out of the way; there was no sign of him. 'Where did he go?' I asked, Lady Mary.

'He's right there, sweetie.' She pointed to a man dressed and looking exactly the same as Justin had; the real shopkeeper. 'If you want to buy something, you should hurry up, darling. Those two men from the club are coming over.'

A jab of fear shot through me and a peek around the items in the shop revealed the two men coming directly for us. Two Ukrainian assassins, hardly the type of person I wanted to spend time with. The police would be here any second, their response to the report of a murder in the club taking no more than a few minutes. I needed to get going.

'Patricia!'

Now what?

Everyone was calling my name today. Everyone seemed to know who I was. The assassins were crossing the street, each of them slipping a hand inside their thin jackets to reach for something. My fear-fuelled senses told me they were going to pull out guns. Would they shoot me and then shoot the police if the police arrived before they could flee?

'Patricia!' Now I recognised the voice. It was Alistair. 'And Lady Mary, what a treat,' he said as he neared us.

I was at panic point, I was trying to keep out of sight of the Ukrainians while simultaneously trying to get Alistair to safety. He saw Lady Mary though, so went to her first.

'Lady Mary,' he greeted my friend, a woman he already knew from her previous time on board the Aurelia, with an air kiss and then nodded a welcome to Jermaine.

I was about to yell that we needed to take cover or run away when I saw the Ukrainian assassins change their minds and alter their course. Two police cars screeched to a stop outside the club, their tyres skipping over the ancient cobbles, though it may have been the half dozen ship's security guards with Alistair that caused them to turn away. I doubted I had seen the last of them.

'I see you brought your entourage,' I nodded to the assembled uniforms behind Alistair. Baker, Bhukari, Schneider, Pippin, and more; all members of the ship's security contingent I had grown to know quite well. 'We really ought to be getting along. Can't wait around here,' I suggested quite pointedly I thought.

Alistair didn't get my meaning though as he carried on speaking conversationally, 'They were just heading for some lunch and walked with me, that's all.' He waved them off as they all bid the captain and me a good afternoon and pleasant break in Malta. Their arrival had been timely, scaring off the assassins, if that's what they were, but them leaving now just exposed us again. If the hitmen were still watching, would they return? The police had gone into the club with some of the staff, but the doorman was still visible in the street and he was looking our way, his eyes drawn by the gaggle of people.

Alistair looked me up and down. 'This is a different look for you,' he said. It was a non-committal method of asking what the heck I was wearing without actually using those words. 'I wouldn't have recognised you were it not for Anna.'

'Yes, today has been interesting so far. I need to get my clothes back actually. They are in a shop around the corner. We really should get going.'

Alistair sucked on his lips. 'I, ah. I have learned it is best to not ask too many questions about what you might be up to, Patricia. So, have you all had lunch?'

I almost got to say, not yet, so let's go, when someone else shouted my name. 'Mrs Fisher!' I couldn't believe it; I was going to get caught by the police for sure and I hadn't even done anything.

Shouting my name this time was the delightful family from earlier; the ones with the missing granny. 'Mrs Fisher,' Sarah Tanner managed as she came to a breathless stop, leaning against the edge of the shop for support as her overweight husband caught up.

Anna had another go at getting to Gary Senior. Her top lip pulled back to expose as many tiny pointed teeth as possible. She was a lovely soft, dopey thing one moment, and a growling ball of potential sausage-shaped death the next. I scratched her ears again until she quietened, but Alistair had moved in to greet them.

'Mrs Tanner,' said Alistair. Of course he knew their names; he knew everyone on board. 'Whatever is the matter?' he asked. Then, before she could answer, he performed a quick headcount of the family. 'Wherever is your mother, Mrs Garland?'

'She's been taken!' Sarah managed between breaths. 'And that woman told us to go to the local police!' she poked an accusing finger at me.

Now Alistair was on rocky ground. I gave him a delightful smile when he cast a look my way, inviting him to disapprove of my advice to them. 'Well... I'm sure that Mrs Fisher intended to help you. Were the local police not forthcoming?'

'No, they blinkin' weren't,' snapped Gary Senior. 'They said what she said,' I got another accusing finger jabbed at me. 'Why does everyone think she just decided to go off on her own?'

Wrong footed by knowing nothing about the circumstances, poor Alistair struggled to make sense of what was going on. I decided to help him. 'Mrs Garland was seen getting into the back of a taxi not long after they came ashore.'

'She's not answering her phone, the taxi driver supposedly dropped her off but no one in any of the shops in that area has seen her. It's sex traffickers,' claimed Sarah. 'You can bet on it. My poor mum's going to be forced into a life of pleasing men in some seedy back alley knocking shop. She's got bad knees you know.' Sarah was all but wailing, laying it on thick to convince Alistair he needed to do something.

Baker and the other members of the security team hadn't got far enough away to escape so they were drawn back now by the commotion the woman made. 'Can we be of assistance?' asked Lieutenant Deepa Bhukari, speaking for the group.

Sarah blew her nose loudly. 'Oh, bless you, my dear. What an angel you are.' Her attention swung back to Alistair. 'Thank goodness your crew are better motivated than the famous detective.'

Alistair leapt to my defence before I had a chance to react. 'Now then, Mrs Tanner, I believe I speak for Mrs Fisher when I assure you this case will be her number one priority. I will assist her and give her the full support of the Aurelia's security team.'

I tugged his sleeve. 'I already have a case,' I whispered in his ear, annoyed that he thought he could speak for me.

I got an apologetic look from him, but it was too late for him to change his mind. He focused his gaze on the crew members attentively awaiting his orders. 'Barker, Bhukari, make contact with the British embassy. Alert them to the missing person and have them contact the local authorities on my behalf. Mrs Tanner, do you have a recent photograph you can provide us with?'

'Um, yes,' she said, fiddling with her phone.

'Pippin, take a copy of that picture to circulate. Schneider, you need to get on to Purple Star's top people and find out who they know at Interpol. If there are human traffickers working this area, they will know about them.' With tasks divided out, the team became a flurry of activity. Young Gary picked his nose and played with his phone.

'Oh, thank you, Captain. Thank you so much,' Sarah was gushing and being tactile, touching his arm and looking like she might hug him.

He took her hands in his. 'Please, try to relax, Mrs Tanner. Your mother is most likely not in trouble. But if she is, we will do our best to return her to you before the Aurelia departs in forty-eight hours.'

'Yes. Thank you so much,' she said again. Then she shot me a quick glare, cuffed young Gary around the back of his head for his dirty habits and ushered her family away.

Alistair watched them go, then turned to find me glaring at him. He was wise enough to know that he had overstepped. He was also political enough to know how to spin it. 'The crew will most likely sew this up before sundown, Patricia. You get the credit for another mystery solved but don't have to do any work. Do you think Mrs Garland was snatched by someone?' His question was intended to make me answer it, rather than hit him with whatever words I had lined up. That wasn't going to work on me though.

Calmly, I said, 'Alistair, I am not a detective. I am not a sleuth. The mysteries I have solved were more by accident than anything else. You and I were supposed to be having a quiet, romantic, couple of days here.' I wasn't exactly telling him off, but I wasn't exactly letting him off either.

'Patricia,' he replied, taking my hand. 'I potentially have a passenger missing. I have to give credence to it until I know something more. And did you not just tell me that you already have a case? Is that why you are in disguise?' He had me there.

'She won't tell us what she is up to,' blabbed Lady Mary unhelpfully.

Alistair eyed me carefully. 'Are you mixed up in something dangerous, Patricia?'

Keeping my expression as neutral as I could, I said, 'I can't say.' As luck would have it, yet again I didn't have to supply a real answer because one arrived in the shape of the doorman and his colleagues. One of them, the man I saw taking out the trash earlier, was on his phone, shouting instructions or directions into it so the police could find us quickly.

In all the nonsense with the Tanners and Alistair and arguing about sex traffickers, I had managed to forget that there was a body across the street and the people in the club thought I did it.

I hung my head and sighed. Running away now wouldn't get me anywhere. I sat down on the step that led into the shop and waited for the police to come running. This afternoon was going to be boring.

Local Police

The local police were actually quite nice about arresting me. I offered no resistance, making sure that Jermaine surrendered peacefully as well, but Lady Mary looked positively over the moon that she was to be cuffed and taken away.

'Now this is more like it, Patricia sweetie,' she said as they explained her rights. The club owner turned up, notified no doubt by the doorman and wanted all manner of charges pressed.

The lead cop started by asking why I did it, probably thinking he could get a big pat on the back for arriving at the station with the murderers in custody and a confession in the bag.

'I didn't,' I said with easy conviction since I hadn't. 'He was already dead when I found him.' It wasn't helping my case that I was wearing a disguise. It made me look guilty, so we were going to the station no matter what evidence I presented at this time. I refused to answer any further questions until I had a lawyer present and they accepted that, though the club owner and the doorman were quite vocal about wanting the police to make me talk.

Alistair did his best to keep the situation calm, introducing himself and then me to make sure the officers knew exactly who they had just taken into custody. As one might expect, my completely ludicrous semi-celebrity status had little impact on them. He also took Anna, promising to keep hold of her and called his security team back, so the police were on their best behaviour under the watchful eyes of so many witnesses. He would meet me at the station shortly with a lawyer. He knew just the person.

I hadn't had lunch, that was the thing bothering me most as I slid along the backseat of the squad car though I caught myself smiling despite the circumstances: how many other people could brag they got arrested two hours after arriving in Malta?

Alistair gave a wave of resilience though his smile betrayed a forlorn look as the police car pulled away with me and Lady Mary in the back. Jermaine got his own car. It surprised me how calm I felt, confident that I would be released within a few hours because Alistair would sort out the mess I had got myself into. However, as the car picked up enough speed for the driver to change out of first gear, my eyes alighted on the two Algerian men. They were watching me, crouched slightly to see into the car as it left the area.

'This is fun,' said Lady Mary. She was looking gleefully out of the window on her side at the people looking in. If her hands had been free, I think she would have waved, much like the Queen going past her loyal subjects.

I rolled my eyes. 'Fun isn't the word I would employ, Mary. If you wanted excitement though…'

'Oh, yes. If they served gin in these things, this would be perfect. Do you think they will hold us for long?' she asked, undoubtedly more worried about when she would get her next cocktail than anything else.

I settled into my seat to get comfortable. 'It's murder, Mary. They won't release us until they are absolutely certain we didn't do it. We could be here all night.'

'All night?' she screeched, genuinely shocked at the concept. 'But that simply won't do.' She leaned forward to talk to the men on the front seats. 'I say. I say, there's been a mistake. Could you let us out now?'

To my surprise, the cop in the passenger seat swivelled around to make eye contact. First with Lady Mary and then with me, shot us both a warm smile and said, 'Yes, of course, ladies.'

We had arrived at the station.

'Here you are, ladies.' The cop kept his fake smile in place. 'Just as requested.'

We were met at the car by more cops from inside as the car stopped around the back of the station where persons in custody were taken inside to be processed out of the way of the public eye. It was all very efficient and quite polite but there was also no avoiding it. Lady Mary persisted with her request to be released but gave up when I told her to.

The cuffs came off; we were inside the station and surrounded by armed officers if we felt like trying something. They dealt with Jermaine first, making note of his name, emptying his pockets and making sure he had no weapons or anything else about his person. They eyed him carefully, no doubt giving credence to the reports of his fighting ability from the club staff.

While waiting patiently in line, I looked about at my surroundings. The station was new looking but was an old building, which suggested a recent refit. The computers were also very new, I noted, the keys on the keyboards not yet shiny from use. A man entered the room while Jermaine's belongings were being catalogued. He was stirring a teacup, a small spoon held daintily between thumb and middle finger of his right hand where the tip of his index finger was missing. He had four bars on his epaulette, which when I glanced at the other officers to check, made him the most senior man present by a stretch. I figured he was the chief.

'Are you the chief of police?' I asked, making my voice sound confident and in control.

He continued stirring for a moment as he watched me carefully, his gaze unwavering. 'My name is Chief Rabat. You are Patricia Fisher, yes? I just received a call from the mayor. Your reach is impressive.' He stopped stirring finally, laying the spoon to one side on his saucer, then crossed the room to speak with the desk sergeant booking us in. Jermaine was finished, his belongings taken so he was escorted to the other side of the room to have his photograph taken. The desk sergeant motioned me forward, the cop standing to my side ready to move me if I resisted.

'Please empty your pockets,' the sergeant requested. They were by far the most polite police I had ever met. I did as required, not wanting to hand over the data storage device, but also certain there was no hope to hide it and any mention of it would just draw more attention to it.

The chief picked it up anyway. 'What's on this?' he asked. My mouth pulled itself into an ugly grimace because I had no idea. 'Check it,' the chief ordered, taking my lack of response to be an unwillingness to answer honestly.

'I wouldn't do that,' I said, which got a raised eyebrow from both men. Across the room, Jermaine turned his head to watch. 'It's encrypted,' I added. 'It might damage your computer.' I was guessing the last bit. Justin told me the data drive wouldn't work on a normal computer, I had no idea what it would do, but I didn't expect the result the police got.

With a frown at me for advising them not to, the sergeant took the thumb drive to a separate computer across the room. A flick of the mouse brought it to life, and he reached down to the tower beneath the desk to plug the device into the drive port. 'Whatever you are protecting will soon be revealed.'

As he fiddled, the chief addressed Lady Mary and me. 'I have a report of a disturbance on Quarry Wharf an hour ago. Two ladies matching your description were arguing in the street with another couple. Something about sex trafficking. Was that you?'

I blew out a breath. 'It was.'

'Patricia was trying to help them,' snapped Lady Mary indignantly. 'They were very rude.'

He flicked his gaze from me to her and back to me. 'And now I find you mixed up in a murder at a club. I'll call it murder without waiting for the results of the investigation since I think it unlikely he plunged an ice pick through his brain by himself.' Whatever he intended to say next was cut off by a string of expletives from the sergeant.

Smoke was pouring from the computer and he was frantically clicking the mouse and jabbing keys on the keyboard. With a final word, which was so colourful I thought exclamation marks were going to appear in the air, he yanked the drive back out of its USB port.

The computer caught fire.

The chief watched impassively, his eyes directed at me to see what reaction I might have as the police officer standing by me to keep me in line, ran across the room to grab a fire extinguisher. With a few squirts the flames were gone but the computer was toast.

Calmly, the chief placed his empty cup and saucer down. 'I guess that's why they insist we have a system not connected to the server to check files on. Would you like to tell me what is on that thing now?' he asked.

Everyone in the room was looking at me, including Jermaine and Lady Mary. 'I don't know,' I gave them an honest answer. Beyond that, I wasn't going to say a word.

The chief narrowed his eyes at me. 'Very well, Mrs Fisher. Your reputation will do you no favours here. I want to know why you are looking into human trafficking in my city and what you were doing next to a body in Club Rhumbla. Until I get some answers, you shouldn't expect to leave.' He spun smartly around on the spot, saying, 'See that she's taken to interview room one,' to his sergeant. Then, without a further word, he left the room by the door he came in through.

'Well, he isn't very nice,' said Lady Mary.

Interview

I hadn't been this side of the interview table for a while and I thought, as the chief did his best to make me uncomfortable by taking his time and being deliberate, that I ought to feel more worried than I did. It was all so familiar, you see. Two and a half months on board a cruise ship would be a relaxing, bordering on boring, time for most people. However, for me it had flown by at breakneck speed as murders, thefts, arrests, and near-death incidents joined the days together in a way I couldn't have imagined. Sitting here now, while the police chief wasted a little more time, I worried that I might miss the adventure when I got back to England. How would I fill the days without someone trying to kill me?

I sniggered to myself, the noise attracting the police chief's attention. 'Something amusing, Mrs Fisher? You do understand that you are under arrest and charged with murder, yes?'

'Oh, yes,' I replied. 'And there's nothing funny about a man getting killed. I didn't do it though and I will not be able to answer any of your questions, I'm afraid.'

'Oh, really?' He made it sound like he accepted my challenge. 'Refusing to cooperate will do you no favours.'

'I doubt speaking without my lawyer present will either. Are you allowed to question me at this time?' Now I was challenging him.

He offered me a congenial smile. 'All we are doing is talking. I'm giving you the opportunity to tell me your side of the story, Mrs Fisher. There are some very suspicious circumstances regarding your first couple of hours on Maltese soil, don't you think?'

I recognised that it was a question, so I didn't answer as I said I wouldn't.

My lack of response wasn't lost on him. 'Mrs Fisher, if you have committed no crime, you will not need legal counsel. I am simply trying to establish what you were doing on Quarry Wharf earlier.'

His statement caught me off guard. He was asking about the incident with the Tanners. A loud discussion on their part from which I walked away. He had a dead body in the morgue with some interesting ear jewellery, why was he asking me about Quarry Wharf? My mouth opened, but I closed it again without speaking.

Unflustered, the chief continued to press. 'This might be really important, Mrs Fisher. I want to put the murder to one side for now. I have yet to determine what happened, but I expect to hear that you are innocent of the crime, or of any crime despite how things look.' He was trying to win me over. 'So my focus is on the suggestion that there is human trafficking occurring under my nose. Mrs Fisher, I am gravely concerned that there is indeed human trafficking going on here: unaccompanied women getting snatched and taken out of the country. My belief is they are transported to Africa, where European women might be considered a more valuable prize. I have an undercover operation in place already, but in just two hours you have stirred up a hornet's nest that may have deep repercussions.'

I sat forward in my chair for the first time. 'Goodness, I had no idea.' I was genuinely worried that I might have negatively impacted a police operation.

'Perhaps not, Mrs Fisher, but I must beg that you desist from pursuing this line of investigation any further. Will you tell me how you came to be looking into this terrible crime?'

Feeling bad now because I had been so uncooperative, I considered what to tell him. 'A woman went missing this morning. An older lady named Nora Garland.'

'And you think she may have been snatched by human traffickers?' the chief asked.

I bit my lip as I wracked my brain and wondered what I thought. 'I don't know. Her family certainly thought so, but I was prepared to dismiss it until now. I expected that she had simply absconded for a little peace and quiet.' I pulled a face. 'They are not a very nice family, you see. I would want to escape them, but my opinion may be wildly inaccurate.'

Chief Rabat sat back in his chair and looked to the ceiling as he thought. That went on for more than a minute though I remained politely quiet until he was ready to speak again. 'What do you plan to do now, Mrs Fisher?'

'Am I free to go?' I asked with my head tilted to one side slightly in uncertainty.

He flipped his eyebrows at his sergeant and got a smirk in response. 'Not yet, Mrs Fisher, no. I wish it were that simple. While I doubt you are the murderer, I still have to follow due process and ask relevant questions. Your... accomplices, partners, whatever they are, are being questioned separately. There is no crime in dressing up, nor in sneaking into a men only club, however, your butler, I believe he said was his position, he attacked and injured several men.'

'He was protecting me,' I protested.

'Yes, Mrs Fisher. Of that I have no doubt, but why would he need to? I have injured persons and a club owner with a dead body. He will lose business, someone is guilty of murder... these things have to be attended to correctly. Jermaine Clarke will be charged with assault; of that you can be sure.'

I wanted to protest more. The concept of Jermaine being incarcerated and then charged was unthinkable, especially since he wouldn't have been there were it not for me. I had no position to argue from though and Chief Rabat knew it.

A knock interrupted whatever he was going to say next. So he said, 'Come,' instead.

A female officer opened the door and stuck her head inside. She was the first female in uniform I had seen thus far. Perhaps a new thing, I wondered, not knowing how progressive Malta was as a nation. She was young and pretty with delicate features and an abundance of wonderful black hair, it was pinned up so it would fit under her hat.

'There's a lawyer here to represent Mrs Fisher and the others, sir. He is very angry that they are being interviewed. He has a man in uniform with him who claims to be the captain of the ship they are travelling on, plus he has a contingent of security from the ship with him and the mayor is here. He is angry too.'

I saw the chief's features change when she said the mayor was here. I guess he was used to dealing with lawyers and such, but the mayor might be the one who appointed public servants like the chief of police.

'Oh,' the young woman continued. 'I have the coroner's initial findings here too, sir.'

He took the offered page of printed paper. 'What does it say?' he asked her even as he read it.

'He estimates the time to death to be somewhere around twelve thirty, sir. The body is too cool for it to be any later in the day than that.'

From across the table, I said, 'So a full two hours before I got to the club.' Then to rub it in, I asked. 'Am I free to go now?'

'Yes, she is,' said a man in a very expensive-looking suit as he barged into the room. 'Come along Mrs Fisher.' He thumped a briefcase down on the desk to draw the chief's attention. 'Shaun O'Donnell, legal representative for Purple Star Cruise lines. I am taking Mrs Fisher with me now. You haven't charged her with anything because you have nothing to charge her with. The murder occurred while she was still on board the Aurelia, a fact that can be corroborated by many witnesses plus CCTV camera footage from the ship's exit. This is an illegal interview…'

'It's not an interview. It is an informal conversation,' the chief argued. 'We are not recording what is being said…'

'To ensure no one can accurately report you bullying my client,' Shaun O'Donnell spoke over the chief as the chief had so rudely done to him just a moment ago. He turned his attention to me. 'Come along, Mrs Fisher, the captain is ready to take you to your hotel.' He beckoned for me with his left hand.

I felt a little unsure, something about everything that was happening was off somehow. However, I rose to my feet and the chief made no move to deter me from leaving. I was indeed free to go it seemed though I would be scratching my head about this for a while yet.

Shaun O'Donnell made sure I left the room first, following me out and pointing back along the corridor so I knew which way to go. I could already hear Lady Mary ahead of me, complaining that she was parched as usual.

Alistair greeted me as I came through a door to find more than half a dozen security guards, plus Alistair and Lady Mary. If the mayor was here, he was somewhere else in the station now. Most likely giving Chief Rabat a stern talking to.

'Are you alright, Patricia?' asked Alistair, giving me a quick kiss on the cheek in greeting. 'I got here as soon as I could.'

I returned the kiss and took a step back so I could see everyone. 'You all did a fantastic job,' I praised them. 'Thank you for mobilizing so quickly.' I looked about in concern though, two important figures were still absent. 'Where're Jermaine and Anna?'

Alistair was quite apologetic when he admitted, 'They are keeping Special Rating Clarke for now.' I opened my mouth to protest, but Alistair stilled me with a hand on my arm. 'O'Donnell from corporate is on it. They have legitimate charges against him, but I expect to be able to get them quashed. It will just take a little longer, I'm afraid.'

I puffed out my cheeks. I knew there was nothing I could do to speed up his release – now was not the time for a jailbreak, but it pained me to know he was in this situation because of me. 'And Anna?' I asked.

'I left her on the ship. I sent a steward to collect her things from your suite and had them taken to the bridge. She was a big hit. When I left, she had about three dozen people fighting to look after her. I don't think you need to worry. Perhaps you and I can have this evening just to ourselves and collect her tomorrow?' he suggested. It made sense, but I had to shout down my rising natural protective instinct. If I couldn't see her, I didn't know if she was safe even though she was usually in far more danger just by being close to me. Alistair had made a decision about her that wasn't his to make. It irked me though I said nothing.

Then my eyes flared as I remembered the data drive! 'I need to get my things back!' I spluttered, spinning around to find an officer to talk to.

'They are being brought out right now,' Alistair assured me. He was right, boxes for Lady Mary and me appearing moments later as two cops came through a door to join us. They had the paperwork with them for us to sign, the transaction taking place in the front reception of the station not the back room we came in through. The difference undoubtedly the influence of the mayor.

The little black data storage device was there, undamaged despite setting a computer on fire. I was still dressed as Sam Spade though, not that I put the hat and wig back on now they were returned to me. 'I need to go back to Old Mint Street. I left my dress and shoes and things in a shop around the corner. Can we do that first?'

Alistair nodded his head, then turned to address the security guys. 'Thank you all for assisting today. Please return to your duties.' As they each replied and started for the door, he called Lieutenant Baker back. 'Has the team had any luck locating Mrs Garland?'

Lieutenant Baker and I had spent many hours together during my time on board the Aurelia. He was probably my favourite of the security team and certainly someone I felt I could rely on. He said, 'No, sir. The Tanner family returned to the ship a short while ago. Schneider continues to liaise with the local police and Interpol. I believe he said Interpol were sending a man. I got the impression they have particular interest in human trafficking in this region.'

Alistair nodded. 'Well done, Lieutenant. Keep up the good work. I want that lady found before we sail.'

'Yes, sir.' Lieutenant Baker saluted his captain, gave me a crisp dip of his head and followed his colleagues outside.

That left just Lady Mary, Alistair and me, all three of us walking toward the doors and the sunshine outside.

'I think I shall head back to the ship,' announced Lady Mary. 'I need to unpack and settle into my suite and I have been in these clothes for far too long; jail cells are not very well air-conditioned, you know?'

Outside was another Purple Star limousine, what Alistair would have arrived in no doubt. 'You should take this, Lady Mary,' he offered. 'Let me get my bags from the back.'

'We can all travel together,' she argued. 'The driver can drop you first.'

Alistair reached in to snag a small travel suitcase, the type they let you have as carry-on luggage on flights. Stepping back, he said, 'The ship and our hotel are in opposite directions. Patricia and I will take a cab. Look there's one right there.' He pointed across the street.

All decided, Lady Mary slipped inside and let the driver close the door for her. By the time we waved it off, she was already dipping into the bar inside.

Finally alone, I was ready to spend a little time with Alistair. Justin the spy said he would contact me later, so there was nothing I could do about the data storage device for now. The missing Mrs Garland was being investigated by the able and competent ship's security team so there was nothing for me to do except tidy myself up, lock the door on our hotel room and stay in bed until we got hungry and ordered room service.

As if reading my thoughts, Alistair cheekily pinched my bum and nudged me toward the cab. 'Come along, saucy. Those men's clothes aren't doing it for me, but I planned to get you out of whatever you were wearing so it will soon make no difference.' Buoyed by the thought, even as my cheeks warmed, and with Alistair acting like a horny juvenile to tease me, we both skipped across the road to jump into the cab. I sat behind the driver, which was a shame, because had I sat the other side, I might have noticed that I knew his face.

Taxi Driver

'Where to, please?' asked the driver as he checked his mirror and pulled away.

I replied as I did my best to take in the sights of Malta sweeping past my window, 'Old Mint Street, please. Close to Club Rhumbla. Then onward to the Excelsior Hotel.'

'Very good. British, are we?' he asked in that universally chatty way you so often get from cab drivers.

I kept my eyes on the impressive ancient architecture of Valetta even as I said, 'I am.'

'There was an incident of some kind at Club Rhumbla earlier today. You're not thinking of going there, are you? I'm not sure it's open.'

I smiled at the cabby's observation, wondering what he would make of the news that I could tell him. He continued to jabber away though neither Alistair nor I were joining in. Alistair's hand found mine across the divide of the backseat and we held hands for a moment, just being together and not needing to talk.

Once again, the ride lasted only a few minutes, the taxi pulling up right out front of Club Rhumbla where police were still visible both inside and outside and the club owner, a man who had pointed me out earlier today, was with them. That made me a little nervous, Alistair picking up on it.

'Which shop do I need to collect your things from?' he asked. I had to turn myself through ninety degrees and lean right across to his side of the car to point the place out. We could just about see it, tucked down a side street out of the way. I got a peck on the lips as he grabbed the door handle. 'I won't be a moment.'

The moment the car door closed the driver spun around in his seat to look back at me. 'Mrs Fisher. You still have the device, yes?'

Startled from my daydreaming thoughts about the pleasant evening ahead, I realised that, yet again, I was looking at Justin Metcalf-Howe. 'How the devil are you the cab driver?'

He shrugged. 'The real cab driver needed a break.'

'A break? Oh, my life. Did you kill him?'

'No. He fell asleep after I covered his mouth in a chloroform-soaked cloth. Wonderful stuff chloroform. Unfashionable now, but I like the classics.' He was actually romanticising the spy business. 'He'll come to in a short while unharmed and sitting in a corner booth of a café where his cab was parked. He'll assume he fell asleep eating his lunch, which I was good enough to pay for, of course.'

'Yeah,' I drawled. 'Anyway, yes I still have the device. Can you take it back now, please?' I took it from my pocket to thrust in his face.

'Goodness, no, Mrs Fisher. There're far too many people following me. I have a new rendezvous point for you. There are catacombs in Mdina. They are well signposted but there will be a lull between tourist groups tomorrow at 0930hrs. You need to enter the catacombs via the emergency exit on the south side. It will be propped open for you. Inside, you will find Wyatt Westridge. He is your new contact. Your code phrase, so you can identify him is, "The stones are always coolest this time of the year." He will reply, "But only those safely tucked underground." Have you got that?'

'What?' I managed to stammer, overloaded by times and information.

'0930hrs. The catacombs in Mdina. South entrance. Wyatt will have a decryption device with him. You can offload the data there directly and be done. Your nation owes you a debt of gratitude.'

Suddenly, he fell quiet and faced the front of the car again, both hands on the steering wheel. A second later, the back door reopened, and Alistair got in with a plastic bag stuffed full of my clothes. 'It took longer than expected because the girl working in there now wasn't there this morning and had no idea what I was talking about. She had to fetch her dad from upstairs. Here you are. You might want to check it's all there.'

I performed a cursory search, decided nothing important was missing and instructed the driver to head to our hotel. The journey to the final point took only ten minutes, the whole thing spent in silence as I tried to commit code phrases, times and directions to memory. At the hotel, Justin the fake taxi driver swung the car into a drop off area set beneath a large awning. A doorman, this one looking elegant in tails and a top hat despite the heat, stepped forward to get my door and welcome us both to the Exclesior Hotel.

Alistair paid Justin, utterly unaware that he wasn't really a cab driver and the British Intelligence spy drove away without even a glance in my direction. I wasn't exactly rattled by his ability to appear when I didn't expect it, but in the hotel's reception I found myself peering at the man behind reception, the chap that came to escort us to our room, a porter going by with a trolley. Despite my scrutiny, none of them turned out to be Justin in yet another disguise.

The room was signed for, a credit card swiped for incidentals and we had a key. Alistair had a gleam in his eye, but my stomach was rumbling audibly as we got in the elevator. 'You missed lunch, didn't you?' he said.

'I was busy getting arrested instead,' I replied with a grin. The porter escorting us to our room cut his eyes at me in the mirrored glass of the elevator doors when he heard what I said and then firmly fixed them staring dead ahead again.

'We will drop our things, let you get changed, and go for an early dinner then. Or a late lunch, if you prefer. No good you being distracted by thoughts of food.'

I wanted to argue, but my stomach gurgled again, the noise loud enough to convince me I ought to feed it. 'Sorry,' I apologised needlessly. I knew he was content to wait an hour.

He put an arm around me. 'I'm hungry too. You might be surprised to hear that I get bored of food on board. I hope the passengers never feel the same, but I have been on board since the ship launched and rarely eat anywhere else. I assumed we would eat well tonight so only had a light lunch. That was several hours ago now.'

The matter settled, I left Alistair to tip the young man, crossed the suite to where my suitcases were stacked, carried one to the bed and found a suitable outfit.

'Did you bring enough clothes, Patricia?' asked Alistair, taking in the stack of suitcases piled on the ottoman. When I looked at him, I got a smirk and a raised eyebrow.

'Jermaine packed for me. He wanted to make sure I had enough clothes to cover any eventuality.'

'He certainly did that. Will you manage when you no longer have him?' It wasn't the first time Alistair had asked such a question. I felt they were aimed at getting me to decide what I was going to do when the ship reached Southampton. He made it clear that he wished for me to stay onboard.

I hooked two fingers through the straps of a pair of sling back heels, hung a dress over my shoulder and paused before I went to the bathroom. 'We should discuss this over dinner,' I offered. It was a big subject. One too big for us to do without both being ready for it. Right now, I needed a quick shower and to get changed. Like Lady Mary, I had been perspiring into my clothes for several hours now and felt less than sexy.

Assuring Alistair that I would not be long, I slipped into the bathroom and left him to wait. Whether it was impatience, or the knowledge that he would be welcome, I wasn't surprised when the echoing sound of the water in the shower changed to tell me the door had opened. A hand touched my right hip and lips grazed my shoulder with a gentle kiss.

'Could you pass the soap, Patricia?'

The Conversation

We found food in a secluded restaurant on a rooftop just across the street; the hotel's concierge earning his tip for recommending it. We were the only ones there, the late afternoon/early evening hour dictating that we missed the late lunchers, and the dinner seekers were yet to arrive.

Alistair ordered an expensive bottle of local wine and a local dish of rabbit in red wine for a starter. It was served with excellent fresh bread, still warm from the oven. With that eaten and waiting for our grilled octopus salads, another local delicacy, I felt that one of us had to broach the subject of where we were going as a couple, so I did it before he could.

'I'm getting off the ship in Southampton,' I told him bluntly.

He took a sip of his wine and looked to the horizon. When he settled the glass back where it had been, he met my eyes. 'You seem very set on that course.'

I took a sip from my own glass. 'I am.'

'I love you, Patricia.' It was a bold statement, but he said the words with absolute conviction, and I believed him. 'I have never met anyone like you, nor do I expect to ever meet anyone like you again. I want you to stay with me on board the Aurelia. The captain's stateroom is designed to hold a family. It is big enough, that's for sure. Will you consider giving it a try? Giving me a try?'

He wasn't even asking that much. He hadn't pushed a five-carat diamond across the table, he wasn't trying to pin me down. Instead, he was taking down all his defensive barriers and expressing himself and his hopes for the future. The problem was that I wanted to get off the ship.

'I can't,' I replied quietly, not meeting his eyes as mine began to well a little. 'My time on board the ship has been incredible, and maybe once I am home, I will feel the need to return. Right now though, all I can think about is getting on with my life. This… silly adventure I am on has to stop. I have never been me.' He cocked an eyebrow as he tried to understand what I was trying to tell him. 'What I mean is, I don't remember a time before Charlie. I was barely more than a child when I met him so my memories of not being married are basically my childhood. I arrived on the ship hopelessly lost as a person but now I have found myself and I need to spend time getting to know who I am. I cannot go from being Mrs Charlie Fisher to being the captain's girlfriend or the captain's wife or whatever we might morph into. I need to be just me for a while. I need to be Patricia Fisher.' I let my words trail off, happy that I had finally managed to articulate how I felt.

The waiter arrived with our main course, which looked and smelled as delicious as it sounded. Neither of us said anything for a while and neither of us picked up our cutlery to start eating. It was a terrible moment, but it was also one that had to happen. Alistair and I were in very different places emotionally. He was open and I was closed. Many might argue that I had found myself an incredible man, and they would be right, but there would be other voices that would question whether I needed a man, or what I needed him for. Sexual pleasure, yes. Company even, though I could achieve company with other women just as easily and have far more to talk about. He was wonderful and I pushed him away in the knowledge that I might regret it, but certain I would regret not finishing my journey and finding myself first.

'I think we should eat,' Alistair said, quietly picking up his knife and fork. 'We still have time together before we reach Southampton.' He looked down, selected a morsel of the grilled octopus and began eating. What he left unsaid, I felt sure, was his intention to change my mind. He was savvy enough to know that suggesting he could would result in my heels digging in.

He was lovely and he was prepared to announce his love for me. I didn't love him in return though, not yet at least, and he deserved better than that.

The octopus was quite delicious.

A Night of Passion

The difficult conversation was behind us and Alistair, thankfully, was mature enough to put it to one side so we could enjoy our evening. I liked him. I liked him a lot and under different circumstances, like if I had never been married or had been divorced for years, I might have leapt at the chance to be his significant other. The timing was wrong for me, but that didn't mean that I was rejecting him right now. There was still time that we could spend together, and that time would be precious to me. Perhaps, when I looked back at it, it would always be time that I considered precious.

With a four-course meal completed slowly and conversation drifting, quite naturally it felt, to other topics, our meal lasted for more than three hours. Other hungers, which might have driven us back to the hotel room sooner, had been sated somewhat by our interlude in the shower. The sun was setting by the time we left the rooftop and other patrons had filled most of the available tables, further upholding the concierge's claims about the restaurant.

Arm in arm, we walked back to our hotel, the distance from restaurant to lobby less than fifty yards and we chatted back and forth the whole way. Alistair had visited the tiny island nation many times on many different ships and considered it to be one of his favourite places. In his opinion, the eclectic mix of so many different nations which visited over the millennia, using it as a stopping off point in the middle of the Mediterranean, made it one of the most diversely interesting places on the planet. I liked to listen to his voice; he was great at telling anecdotes, but we were taking the stairs back to our suite on the second floor and once the door shut we were probably going to stop talking in favour of other activities.

As we paused to open the door, I still had my arm linked through his. I reached up to cup his chin and turn his mouth toward mine. I kissed him quickly as the door lock beeped. 'I need the bathroom,' I let him know, just in case he planned to grab me and throw me on the bed when the door opened.

He pushed the door open and let go of my arm, kissing my cheek and neck as he stood aside to let me go in.

As I pushed open the bathroom door, I heard him call out, 'I'll be waiting.' It put a smile on my face as I closed the door behind me. I was in for a pleasant evening, or maybe that should be a pleasing evening. The correct terminology was unimportant. I was excited about sex for the first time in years; that in itself was important and arguably something to be cherished.

A few minutes later, and not wanting to make him wait any longer, I had applied a touch more perfume, changed into the little negligee I squirreled away in here before we went out and I was making growling faces in the mirror to gee myself up. I was going to give him a night he would never forget.

Making sure the light from the bathroom would silhouette me, I threw it open to announce my presence and struck a pose against the doorway, my toes pointed to accentuate the muscle in my legs. The message from my eyes took a moment to reach my brain.

The room was almost completely black but there was enough moonlight coming in for me to see that Alistair wasn't on the bed waiting for me. Alistair wasn't even in the room.

My mouth was hanging open in surprise that he wasn't there, but my confusion quickly changed to utter terror when I saw the two Algerian gentlemen sitting by the window. So complete was the shock effect, that I almost collapsed from the fright.

Neither spoke, both content to study me, only their eyes moving as they silently watched me recover from the surprise. I had no doubt it was the same two men from earlier, they were even wearing the same clothes.

'What do you want?' I demanded. 'Where is Alistair?'

One was sitting on the dressing table stool, the other sat on the edge of the dressing table itself though I couldn't determine what the hierarchy was or even if there was one.

'He is safe. For now,' said the one on the stool. He was wearing a dark blue suit, with a crisp white shirt and white tie. He looked like a CEO, if one judged that a person's success could be seen in their clothes. I knew it couldn't, but the analogy still worked.

'What does that mean?' I asked, desperately scared for what had happened to him.

'It means, Mrs Fisher, that you need to keep your head down and your nose out of other people's business. If you do that, we will return him before your ship is due to sail. If you do not, we will kill him and mail parts of Alistair Huntley to his family for the next year.'

It was quite an effective threat. One that made my knees feel weak.

A knock at the door interrupted any further conversation. 'Room service.'

My eyes were locked on the two Algerian men. They hadn't shown any weapons until now, but both drew a small calibre pistol from a holster inside their jackets, the one on the stool nodding to the one on the table to check the door. At least now I knew who was in charge.

I was still frozen to the spot, terror preventing me from shouting a warning to whoever was at the door, but as the lower ranking man went to the door with the gun in his hand and ready to fire, I bit down on my fear and forced oxygen into my lungs so I could shout.

However, a bullet came through the door to hit the Algerian before I could give my warning. I recognised the suppressed sound it made meant it had been fired through a silencer. That alone told me the person outside firing in was another spy or assassin or something. The Algerian man took a step back in shock, his eyes staring down at his chest, but a second, third, fourth and more bullets hit him, and he fell dead to the carpet. The man on the stool was up and moving by the time his partner fell, but the door opened inwards suddenly, the click of the lock being opened almost lost amid the reverberating sounds of silenced gun fire.

A woman's figure was silhouetted for just a heartbeat in the doorframe before it vanished into the shadows of the room. Two more shots rang out and the other Algerian man dropped to the carpet. The woman's shadow flashed across a window, appearing briefly and then vanishing again but I heard the skittering noise of a gun being kicked across the floor.

Then a lamp came on to throw light across the room.

'Get dressed,' the woman said. 'We have to leave.'

A Very British Spy

Still too stunned to move, I managed to stutter, 'Who are you?' at the young woman. She was somewhere around thirty years old, with shoulder length, lustrous brunette hair braided into a French plait that reached just beneath her collar. At almost six feet, she was tall, and she was also lean; tall and skinny some might say, but men would find her attractive for certain. Her accent was Chelsea or Kensington; one of the posh parts of London where a garage would set a person back a swift million. She sounded like private education and money.

I watched her as she moved quickly to the windows, furtively checking out of each of them without getting close enough to reveal herself, then turned to address me. 'I'm a friend of Justin's. He was concerned for your safety and asked me to make sure you reached your rendezvous tomorrow.' She indicated the two dead men on my hotel room's carpet using the silencer end of her pistol. 'Clearly, he was right to worry.'

'Wha...' I was on complete overload. I couldn't make coherent thoughts link in my head. My boyfriend was missing and there were two dead men on the floor a few yards from me. This was extreme circumstances even by my recent standard. Struggling to focus, I managed to form a sentence. 'I'm going to need a little more than that.'

'We don't have time for this,' she snapped, as she grabbed some clothes from one of my suitcases and threw them at me. 'These two are not the only ones after the device you have. You do have it, don't you?' I didn't move and I didn't answer. I had no idea who she was, and I was quite certain I didn't want to go with her. Sensing my hesitancy, she softened. 'They have your boyfriend?'

'They said they did,' I murmured.

She nodded and blew out a breath. 'My name is Emily Hughston-Roberts. I am British Intelligence just like Justin. I was assigned to track him down when he went missing in Greece a few days ago. That led me to Malta where he left a coded message for me to get me to you.' On the carpet, the boss man of the two Algerians groaned and shifted slightly. She shot him again just for good measure. 'I think they are Algerian military. Everyone wants what you have on that device. You won't be safe, and they won't let your boyfriend go until you have safely passed it on.'

'Why would they let him go then?' I asked. I thought it far more likely they would just kill him.

'They won't,' she admitted. 'We will have to find a way to rescue him, but the data on the device has to take priority. Letting it fall into the wrong hands could cost the lives of millions of innocent people.'

I shook my head with bewilderment. 'What is on the drive?'

'The less you know about it the safer you will be.' Our eyes met for a moment, then she tucked her gun away and picked up my clothes, unfolding a shirt for me to put on and holding it out like she was trying to dress a child. 'We must hurry. They could have back up.'

Galvanised into action, I did as she urged me to, tore off the wasted negligee and quickly got dressed. No sooner had I got my shoes on, than she was grabbing my hand and tugging me to the door. 'What about my things?' I asked, digging my feet in to hold her back.

'No time, and no space in my car.' She tried to pull me along and she was stronger than me, her body mostly muscle and twenty-five years younger than mine.

I tore my arm free. 'I still need a few things.' I hadn't even checked my phone was in my handbag yet. I took ten seconds, with Emily tapping her foot and checking left and right along the corridor the whole time. My rushed mental checklist made sure I had on appropriate clothing: jeans, ankle boots, a shirt, and a short jacket, and that I had my phone and the damned data storage device. I stuffed a spare pair of knickers in for good measure and let the rest of it go; I would just have to manage without it. Then I changed my mind at the last moment, grabbed the bag on top of the pile and hooked it over my arm.

At the door, Emily said, 'Stay behind me.'

'Why is it so dark?'

'Because I killed the lights,' she whispered. 'Try to keep as quiet as possible. There may yet be more of them here.' Then she crept along the corridor to the stairs, her footsteps somehow silent where mine echoed each time I moved. Trying to make less noise, I was so focused on my feet that I didn't see her stop and bumped into her.

As I was drawing a breath to apologise, she clamped a hand over my mouth, her eyes wide to convey a message of urgency. 'Someone's coming,' she whispered, her mouth right next to my ear to make as little noise as possible. 'Back up.'

Concentrating to hear what she could, all I got was silence. 'I don't hear anything,' I questioned her.

Once she had backed me up a few yards and pushed me into the alcove formed by a door, she said, 'Exactly. If it were people coming back from a night out, they would be making more noise. Whoever is coming up the stairs is moving as stealthily as they can and that means they are probably here to kill you.'

My pulse hammered in my head, the sound of it almost deafening as I listened and waited. Emily was pressing against me, her hard, lean body trying to get into the same alcove as me and also form a human shield should there be any shooting. As two shadows reached the top of the stairs and stepped out, they were framed by moonlight coming in the window behind them at the end of the corridor.

Emily stepped forward and shot them both. Two bullets each to their centre of mass. The noise the gun made with the suppressor fitted was still loud in the corridor but not loud like a gun shot. It sounded more like a champagne bottle opening under pressure. Their bodies falling made more noise, and yet again Emily was grabbing my arm and yanking me forward.

'Let's go,' she insisted at normal volume. I had to step over the two bodies lying on the carpet but gasped when I recognised them. It was Bogdan and Yuri, the two Ukrainian assassins. 'You recognise them?' she asked, pulling me down the stairs.

I hurried my feet to keep up with her. At the pace she was going, I would trip and fall if I wasn't careful. 'They tried to get the data storage device from me earlier today,' I told her.

At the bottom of the stairs, she swung her gun left and right, decided the coast was clear and hurried toward the front of the hotel. 'They won't try it again.'

Her words echoed in my head as I realised that was five bodies in one day plus two kidnappings. Not that I thought Nora Garland's disappearance was linked to the spy thing going on, but the police, who had been forced to release me earlier today, were going to find two more bodies in my hotel room and yet another kidnapping if they were able to work out that Alistair was missing.

I thought we were on our way to the hotel lobby to leave by the front doors, but Emily had other ideas. Using a door card, she opened a room, tugged me into it and went to the windows on the far wall. I figured it was her room until a shocked couple sat up in bed, the woman pulling the covers up to her neck. I couldn't help but look at them, trying to apologise as Emily opened the window and climbed out.

'Come along, Mrs Fisher, we must hurry,' she insisted as I said sorry to the couple yet again.

The drop to the pavement outside was seven or eight feet. She let go of the frame and landed with the grace of a cat. I threw my bag out, then jumped after it, caught the back of my jacket on the latch to lock the window, fell, stopped, hung in the air for a second until my jacket ripped and then landed in a crumpled pile by her feet.

'Ow,' I groaned as I rolled over to get my hands and feet underneath myself.

Emily was eyeing me dubiously as if I was messing about and playing the clown on purpose. 'Are you quite alright, Mrs Fisher?'

I grabbed her shoulder as I straightened myself up. 'Yes, thank you. I'm just getting on a bit and jumping out of windows isn't something life has prepared me for.'

I got an odd look in response. Then she started walking again, toward the rear of the hotel and the dark backstreet I could see there. 'My car is around the corner,' her voice echoed off the tall stone buildings.

Giving a sore knee another rub, I set off after her in a limping shuffle. But a shout from behind made me run.

Wanted

In the dark, I couldn't see who it was behind me, but with the body count rising, I wasn't inclined to hang around for introductions. 'Hurry,' Emily yelled, her shout followed immediately by the sound of an engine roaring to life.

Fast footsteps were chasing me along the road, but no one was trying to shoot me yet. At the corner, I grabbed a drainpipe to throw myself around it and spotted Emily's car idling at the curb. She was in the driver's seat, one arm hanging over the door as she turned around to beckon me.

The car was a small convertible, an Alpha Romeo I thought, though I had never been very good at remembering car brands or models. I ran around to the passenger side, throwing my bag in as I went, but had barely got my bum into the seat when she mashed the pedal to the floor and took off like a scalded cat. Risking a glance over my shoulder, I saw two men hurtle around the corner and into the space her car had just left. Seeing they had been beaten, both men pulled guns from inside their coats.

With a spike of adrenalin, I ducked my head and peeked between the two seats. My limited view was enough to see them accept that we were out of range, then they were lost from sight as Emily whipped the low-slung car around a corner.

'Oh, my life,' I gasped in ragged breaths from the exertion and the excitement. 'Who were they?'

In contrast to me, with my hair all over the place and my clothing skew-whiff from putting it on too fast and then running, Emily looked ready to parade down a catwalk somewhere. She wasn't even out of breath from running and had just killed four men. Surely some of that stuff should wrinkle her clothing or mess up her immaculate hair?

'They were not our friends,' she replied, not actually answering my question. She checked her rear-view mirror and slowed her pace, settling into traffic as she left the back street and joined a main road as it wound its way north from Valetta. 'You should settle in,' she advised. 'But you will have to tell me where we are going. Not the exact location. Just ballpark for now will do.'

'Mdina,' I told her, feeling safe to do so because she wasn't trying to get the final destination from me.

'Then you should definitely settle in. It will take us a while to get to Mdina.' The warm night air swirled around the open-topped car as my scrambled brain tried to unravel all that had occurred in the last few hours. Since stepping off the ship at noon, my butler, Jermaine, had landed in a jail cell, my boyfriend had most likely been kidnapped by an Algerian military outfit, whose lead men were now dead and I was almost certainly wanted in questioning for four deaths. Possibly five as they might now wish to rethink the likelihood that I was not involved in the first one in Club Rhumbla.

Emily focused on driving; the road noise created by having no roof making conversation difficult. I stayed inside my own head, trying to work things out and make some kind of plan to get Alistair back safely. At some point I fell asleep because when I next opened my eyes the sky was beginning to lighten, and I had no idea where I was.

I was still in the car, that was something to be glad about, but Emily wasn't in the driver's seat. A jolt of panic shot through me as I questioned whether I had been duped. Grabbing my handbag from the floor between my feet, I rummaged through the contents, couldn't find what I wanted so upended it in my haste.

The little black data storage device tumbled out with everything else and came to rest on top of the spare pair of knickers I threw in at the last moment. In the horror-filled few seconds when I thought Emily had taken it, I hadn't drawn a breath, so now I gasped in a heaving lungful of air, relieved that she probably was who she said she was.

There was still no sign of her, and I needed to pee now that I was awake. The car was in a parking space behind a building but could have been anywhere in Malta. As far as I could see in every direction, blocky, square buildings dominated. They looked like houses, though I felt the building we were parked behind was more likely to be a business of some kind.

Just as I got out of the car, a door in the back wall of the building opened and Emily came out of it. She looked refreshed and ready for the day, her clothes changed from last night as she now wore a long summer dress in a pastel yellow with a thin brown belt around her waist, plus matching shoes and a wide-brimmed hat. 'Good morning,' she beamed. 'There's a restroom inside with a sink if you want to freshen up.' She held the door for me.

'Where are we?' I asked, twisting and stretching to force the kinks out of my back: I was too old to be sleeping in cars.

'About five miles south of Mdina. We arrived a few hours ago. It's quiet and we are tucked well out of sight. We'll push on to Mdina and get some breakfast when you are ready.'

I thanked her and slipped inside the building, noting the forced lock as the door swung shut; she had broken in. Coming back out a few minutes later, I found that she had turned the car around and was ready to go. The sun was coming up and maybe today I would finally get rid of the stupid device in my handbag that was getting so many people killed. Getting that done wouldn't get Alistair back though. I was certain of that, so there had to be some kind of plan for the British spies to rescue him.

I decided to quiz her on it. 'Get in,' she said, leaning across to push the door open.

I pushed it shut again. 'How are we going to rescue Alistair?'

'One problem at a time, Mrs Fisher. The most important thing is to make sure the data you have is safely passed on.'

'That's not good enough for me, Emily. That sounds like no plan at all. What will have happened to the bodies in my room? Are the police now after me? Who else is trying to get hold of this data device? Justin said everyone would want it.'

Emily produced a gun from her handbag and pointed it straight at me. Yet another jolt of adrenalin flooded my body, making me feel woozy all over again. 'Mrs Fisher, the only reason I haven't shot you and taken the device to the rendezvous myself is because you won't tell me where it is. My mission is to get the data to the decryption device. Keeping either one of us alive beyond that point is an entirely secondary concern. I know what is at stake and will give my life to protect my country. Now get in the car and no more questions about boyfriends.'

Emily was quite scary. Which is to say that she did a good job of scaring me. I opened the door and got into the passenger seat. What other choice did I have?

'Now, you are going to have to tell me where in Mdina we need to go,' she demanded, putting the car in gear and pulling away.

I said, 'Yes,' but didn't give her any more information. The bottom line was that I knew nothing about her. She claimed to be Justin's colleague, and both looked and sounded the part, but I was somehow caught up in a game of spies and had no idea who I could trust.

'Well?' she prompted.

'There's an outdoor marketplace in the town's central square.' It was a complete guess. I had no idea if there would be an outdoor market, or even if Mdina had a square. European towns and cities have a pattern to them, I had found. A large open space in what would have been the ancient central business district occurred regularly, the influence of European settlers crossing the Atlantic or travelling to the Indian Ocean or beyond meant the practice was mirrored in many Caribbean towns and other places too. 'The contact is meeting me just beyond that.'

Using my phone, I was desperately trying to pull up a map of Mdina to work out where the catacombs were. If I could, I was going to lose Emily somewhere, make the drop and hide until I could safely flag down a cab to take me back to the ship. Then I would work out how to find and rescue Alistair. I found the catacombs; they were clearly labelled on the map and a street over from the real town square I only thought I had invented. This was working out better than expected.

Getting Emily's attention, I showed her the map on my phone, her eyes flicking down for a second and back up to the road. 'I'm surprised they didn't pick the catacombs to meet in,' she commented. 'That would be a far safer choice.'

The little black Alpha Romeo left a cloud of fine dust as it left the town of Ghar Barka, but as promised, Mdina was only a few minutes away, the gap between the towns filled with fields of vegetables fighting hard to survive in the parched landscape. Like so much of Malta, there was nothing to see except more barren orangey-brown rock and sand. How they grew anything was a mystery to me.

'We have time to kill,' Emily announced as she swept through the streets of Mdina. To our left and right, tall buildings sprouted toward the sky. 'Let's get some breakfast.'

I offered no argument to her suggestion; I was hungry and thirsty and the early morning streets were filled with the smells of baking bread or freshly brewed coffee. My stomach gave a quiet growl as she swung the car around and into a parking space facing an eatery. It was clearly a tourist area, lots of hotel signs and restaurants around.

Emily was already getting out of the car before the engine had died. I was slower, but I spotted something as I clambered out of my seat. The business next door to the deli place we were heading for wasn't open yet, but it gave me an idea. On the pavement, Emily waited impatiently for me, checking her watch and selecting one of the tables on the street as soon as I moved to join her. She waved the waiter over, her long slender arm getting his attention. 'Coffee, please.' She looked across at me.

'Yes, please,' I replied to her unspoken question.

With her head in her menu, she said, 'Make that two coffees. We'll have a food order for you in just a moment.'

The man scurried away, just as a young woman brought us a pitcher of water. She set it down and turned over the glasses set in front of us. I immediately picked up the jug and started pouring. 'It must take a lot of water to keep your skin looking so good in these harsh environments,' I said conversationally, placing a glass of water by her hand.

She thanked me in an absent-minded way and drank some. I refilled it. Presently the waiter came back with two coffees, a strong dark brew laced with an industrial hit of caffeine. We both ordered egg dishes and I put more water in Emily's glass as she drained what she had.

Less than a minute later, exactly as I hoped, she excused herself. The moment she was out of sight in the restroom in the back, I ran to the shop next door. It was one minute to nine and they still weren't open, but I could see the proprietor moving about inside.

I hammered on the glass, putting a hand above my eyes to shield the glare as I pressed my face to the window to see inside. I saw him wave to me and squint across the room at a clock I couldn't see. Then he shrugged and made his way to the door. There were three deadbolts to undo and a security lock of some kind, plus a steel mesh grill that sat inside the glass. When finally it opened, I held up the data device. 'Do you sell these?' I asked as quickly as I could, hoping to impart my urgency.

He leaned his head back so he could focus his eyes on it; I put it too close for him to see it clearly. 'Yes, we have mass storage devices of all kinds.'

'Yes, but do you have one like this?' I pressed.

'Well, let me see.' He guided me to a rack of them, all hanging in little carboard-backed plastic pouches. I forced my eyes to track across them as fast as I could, grabbed one that looked very similar to the one in my hand and yanked out my purse. Jermaine, the sweetie that he is, made sure some of my dollars were changed into local currency everywhere we went. Malta was no exception, so I checked the price, handed over a bill big enough to cover it and ran for the door as I yelled my thanks to the shopkeeper.

I must have seemed like a mad woman as I hurtled to the door, stopped and slowly peered around the front edge of the building to see if

Emily was back in her seat and then nonchalantly sauntered back to my chair as if nothing had occurred during her absence.

'Your change?' the shopkeeper's voice drifted out after me, but I was taking my seat and trying to look innocent by then.

Emily reappeared, weaving through the tables inside the deli as she came back to our table. 'Are you alright, Mrs Fisher?'

'Yes, why?'

She frowned a little. 'You looked… flustered.'

'Ha!' I forced a laugh. Then lowered my voice. 'In the last twenty-four hours I have seen five dead bodies, four of which you shot. For all I know you killed the fifth too. I have been shot at, arrested, my boyfriend has been kidnapped, and I am about to go looking for a spy in a catacomb to hand over a device which everyone tells me contains details of a new super-weapon which could kill millions. Yes, I'm flustered.' I delivered the lie well because it was all true, it just wasn't the current reason why I looked flustered.

Her frown deepened though. 'The spy is in the catacombs?'

Oh bother.

'I can usually tell when people are lying, Mrs Fisher. It is why I am so good at my job and why I am still alive. You managed to fool me though I cannot decide whether I am impressed by you or should question whether I can trust you.'

Our breakfasts came to break the stalemate stares across the table.

Picking up her knife and fork, Emily said, 'I will come into the catacombs with you.'

'I am expected alone.'

'The contact will not know I am there.'

I believed her, but I couldn't say I was enthralled at the prospect of having her watch me. Any hope of throwing her off my tail or losing her were now gone because she knew where I was going; my big mouth giving away the secret at the last moment.

I sulked for the rest of breakfast, angrily scraping up the last bits of egg and silently moaning at myself. Two minutes later, it was time to go. Emily placed currency under her coffee cup and stood up.

Suddenly, I was nervous, but she grabbed my right elbow in a vicelike grip. 'It's nearly over, Mrs Fisher,' she whispered insistently. 'Once the contact has the device, we can focus on getting Alistair back.'

'Okay,' I growled in reply, yanking my arm back and wondering if it would bruise where her fingers dug in. 'We need to approach from the south. There will be an emergency exit there propped open for us to slip in through. Where will you be?'

With a half-smile, she said, 'I'll be in the shadows.'

Leaving the car where it was in front of the deli for collection later, we set off, me leading with Emily walking ten yards behind so we didn't look to be together if anyone was watching. I glanced around as much as I dared, trying to see if there were any faces tracking my progress along the street; there were none.

Or, rather, there were, I just couldn't see them.

Catacombs

When I looked around to see how far back Emily was, there was no sign of her at all. I paused, caught myself doing it, and hurried on, my pace quicker now because I wanted to get it over with and because arriving late yesterday, the contact in Club Rhumbla was dead. I would have found him dead even if I had been on time yesterday but nevertheless, I wanted to be punctual today.

The south side was easy to find; my phone had a compass function on it, so I only walked by the emergency exit I needed once. I found the door had been propped open with a small rock to prevent it from clicking shut again. I slipped my fingernails around the edge, pulled it open just enough to squeeze through, and slipped inside.

It was dark inside. Of course, it was dark inside. I told myself off for being silly, ducked my head as I went down the steps and put my sunglasses in my handbag. With my hand already inside, I rooted about to find the thumb drive and found two because I had bought a new one. It was a trick from a spy film I must have watched years ago which meant I now had a dummy device I could give someone if they demanded it. Buying it, I had wondered if it might be Emily who was going to turn out to be a double agent or a foreign government spy but thus far she hadn't tried to get the device from me at any point.

I took both devices out of the bag so I could make sure I was handing over the right one, but now I was staring at them and cursing myself. I couldn't tell which was which. They were both brand new, shiny black mass data storage devices. They were different, but the differences were subtle, and I didn't remember which one was the original. There was a dummy here alright and it was me.

A footfall echoed in the dark, the suddenness of the sound made me want to run away. Delivering the device was my only task though – my country would owe me a debt of gratitude. They could keep it. I just wanted this business done and Alistair back.

Convincing my feet to take me around the next corner, I found a man in a suit waiting for me. In his hand he held a squat black box, like the hardened cases people carry expensive or delicate electronic hardware around in. This had to be Justin's contact, Wyatt Westridge.

Nervously, I delivered my line, 'The stones are always coolest this time of the year.'

A smile flickered across his face. 'But only those safely tucked underground.' I had been holding my breath, I realised as I exhaled and drew a gulp of badly needed air. He also seemed to relax, crouching down to place the box he carried on the ground. The catacombs were carved from the bedrock beneath the town. What they had been dug for and the story behind them would be an interesting tour if I were able to be here as a normal tourist. Such things evaded me though.

Light shone outward from the box as a screen inside came to life. 'You have the device?' he asked, holding a hand up so I could pass it to him.

I had one in each hand, gripping them tightly. I still didn't know which was which but now I was going to have to hand one over. 'Funny story...' I started.

I didn't get to finish though because I saw the man freeze and reach for a gun inside his jacket.

'No, no,' said Emily, appearing next to me with her gun pointing directly at the man's head. 'Take it out slowly and toss it.' Her instruction was ambiguous, but we all knew she meant the gun, so he did as she said, deliberately and carefully pulling the gun out between two fingers. It thumped against the hard-packed ground by her feet where he threw it.

Emily said, 'Pick it up, Mrs Fisher.' Once again, her instruction left me in no doubt about what she might do if I failed to comply. I bent to collect it, the gun dangling from my fingers the same way it had from the man's.

Then she shot him. Once, twice. Two bullets into his chest and he fell backwards.

'I had to wait for him to open it, you see? The decryptor has a fingerprint entry system and the device isn't much good without the gear to decrypt it. My instructions were to recover the device, but I like to give value for money. Taking them both things will save someone else a job. Now give me the device,' she demanded, pointing her gun at me now for emphasis.

I hated having guns pointed at me. This time was no exception and the suddenness of it made me drop the man's gun I had been holding.

Emily held out a hand for me to put the device into, and just as I was about to, we both heard someone enter the dark passageway behind us. Her gun swung around to cover the new threat as two men came into sight, both of them carrying guns of their own. Both were pointed in her direction, which took the threat away from me, but I had no sense of reprieve because they could only be here for the super-weapon plans I was carrying.

Then, as they came silently forward, I realised I knew who they were. It was Bogdan and Yuri the two Ukrainian assassins I met in Club Rhumbla. The two who Emily shot dead last night.

'I told you this would work,' Emily bragged to them. All three lowered their weapons. I had been suckered from the start but now I didn't know what was true.

'Has Alistair even been taken?' I asked.

Emily laughed, the sound a high trill. 'Listen to her, boys. That's love right there. She's about to get killed in a dark underground passageway and her only thoughts are for her missing boyfriend.' She laughed again and held her hand out to me once more. 'The device?'

I gave her the one in my right hand. It was fifty-fifty whether it was the right one or not so maybe I would have the last laugh when she discovered later it was the blank one I bought half an hour ago.

'Thank you, Mrs Fisher. You played your part very well. As for your dear Alistair: I have no idea where he is or what might have happened to him. The two men I killed in your room might have been Algerian or might not have. I made the whole thing up on the spot. We were watching from across the street so saw them in your room, hatched a quick plan and fitted my gun with blanks at the bottom of the magazine. Easy really. The papers talk about you as some kind of super sleuth, but I guess you just got lucky a couple of times.'

That was exactly what I kept telling people, but I doubt it was what they would put on my grave after they found my bullet-riddled body.

The popping sound of a suppressed gun echoed loudly in the tight confines of the catacomb. It made me flinch and question if I had just been shot. One of the five-day-stubble guys pitched forward before I could reach a decision about myself, falling dead to the floor as his partner and Emily looked about in a startled reaction.

'Bogdan?' yelled the man still standing, though concern for his fellow ruthless killer seemed out of place. His face bore an angry sneer and his gun arm was coming up directly in line with my face.

I squeaked in fright and ducked just as he started firing. Emily was shooting too, both of them sending bullets down the passageway, back to where the British spy still lay dead on the ground with the decryption device next to him.

One glance was all I needed to convince me I had to run for it or die where I was. The passage leading back to the emergency exit on the south side was two yards away. All I had to do was throw myself in that direction and pray I dodged the deadly bullets going back and forth.

Yuri got hit, a yelp from him drawing my eyes, but he was still shooting. At the other end, whoever they were shooting at got hit, a body I could only just see, falling forward into the passageway.

Emily shouted something in a different language, darted forward to grab the decryption device and I took my chance to get out of the catacombs, snagging Wyatt's gun from by my feet as I ran.

The shooting started again the moment I moved; the man Yuri shot clearly not the only one down there. I left them all behind me, sprinting for the exit and slamming into it as I burst through and back out into the sunshine. Terror propelled me onwards, only the sound of Emily shouting instructions making me look back to see if I might be safe. She and Yuri were also outside, Yuri stopping to jam a handy boulder against the door to keep it closed.

I didn't think they had seen me, but I hid behind a low wall, peering through some weeds so I could see which way they were heading and pick a different direction. They both paused, looking back at the door, their guns pointed at it to kill anyone that attempted to come through. She had the decryption device in her left hand and the data storage device with the weapon plans on it somewhere in her handbag. She might have all the pieces she needed.

I looked at the little black data device I still held, swore at myself and tossed it in my own bag.

Emily decided they were not going to be followed, lowered her gun and put it away and she ran across the dusty ground to reach a car across the street. It was a big four by four Japanese thing and must have been what Yuri and Bogdan arrived in having followed us here. Yuri went with her, blood coming from a wound to his left shoulder, they were going to get away though and there was nothing I could do about it. Then I remembered the gun. Wyatt threw Emily his gun and I ended up with it in my handbag. I yanked it out victoriously, determined to stop them, I was going to shoot their car. I was going to shoot their car and run away, though a little voice in my head said that what I ought to do was shoot both of them from behind the car, catch them completely by surprise, take the other data storage device and the decryptor and escape in Emily's car.

The gun wobbled in my hand as I considered executing two people. I wasn't the type of person that shot other people, even people who were only too happy to kill and might be guilty of causing genocide if not stopped. There was my choice: they had a weapon that could kill millions. If I was prepared to believe that, then I had to accept the task I faced. Hating myself, I brought the gun up to take a shot. I had to shoot two people to save millions.

The car exploded.

One moment Emily was tearing her handbag off her shoulder and diving into the car, the next second, the whole car lifted three feet off the ground as it became a ball of exploding gases. All the glass blew out, the sunroof flew into the air and I was picked up by the shockwave to be thrown backwards. I tumbled along the street.

Had I been closer, the blast would have killed me. Had there been something behind me, colliding with it might have done the same. Battered, bruised, cut in several places from flying glass and covered in dust and grime, I was still alive. Then, just as I thought my heart couldn't handle any more surprises, Emily's handbag landed between my legs to make me jump with fright once more. It was on fire, but the contents spilled out on impact, the device I gave her and the keys to the Alpha sliding across the road to stop by my left hand.

I couldn't help but take a second to look up at the sky. If God was up there, and this was his way of giving me a helping hand, he needed to look up the word benevolent.

Sirens were already echoing in the distance as I pushed myself off the ground. Limping slightly, and looking like a refugee, I started back toward Emily's car. I was more confused than ever, and I still had the stupid data device.

Now though, I needed to get some help and I knew just who to call.

The Team

I got a lot of looks on my way back to the deli where Emily left her car. She didn't need it now, that I was quite certain of. The waiter at the deli saw me in my battered, dirty state and rushed to help, undoubtedly wondering what could have possibly happened to me in the twenty minutes since breakfast. I waved him off, dealing with my most pressing need which was to vacate the area.

The car felt unfamiliar, but they drive on the left in Malta which made the differences between this car and any other I had driven fairly small. I didn't even need a map because the very first sign I saw had Valetta listed on it: It was a small island, after all.

Once out of the town and away from anyone who might be involved in the insanity my life had become, I pulled over at a resting place and took out my phone.

I had to choose who to call; I had several options which were all kind of the same option, but I picked Lieutenant Deepa Bhukari and thumbed the button to connect my phone to hers.

'Oh, my goodness, Mrs Fisher is that you?' She sounded both relieved and surprised to hear from me.

I guessed the news of the bodies in my room had reached the ship. 'Hello, Deepa. Is Alistair there?' I asked hopefully.

'Goodness, no, Mrs Fisher. We were hoping he was with you. The police are all over us, wanting to know if we have seen or heard from either of you. Chief Rabat has been going nuts and accusing us of harbouring you both. He says you killed two men in your hotel room last night. They are trying to force Purple Star Lines to let them search the ship for you.'

'You should let them,' I replied. 'Purple Star can win this one easily by just cooperating. Chief Rabat and his officers can waste hours or days searching the Aurelia. I'm not on it.'

I heard other voices in the background and Deepa said, 'Hold on, Mrs Fisher. I'm going to put you on speaker phone.' There was a moment of dead zone where I got no noise at all and then she was back.

'Mrs Fisher?' said a familiar voice. 'This is Lieutenant Baker.'

'Hi, Patty,' Barbie called out to let me know she was there.

Then Deepa cut in again. 'There are too many of us here to list. We formed a taskforce to try to work out what is going on.'

'Have you got anywhere yet?'

Deepa sighed. 'No, Mrs Fisher. We weren't prepared to believe that you or the captain killed anyone, so we figured the two of you were lying low while you solved the case. If the captain isn't with you, where is he?'

'I wish I knew.' I was thinking fast now, my brain tying to piece together what I had seen and heard in the last day. 'Look, I gain nothing by coming back to the Aurelia. The police will most likely arrest me on sight and worry about proving my guilt later. Can you get to me?'

Barbie said, 'Of course, Patty. Just tell us where you are.'

I shook my head as I wriggled my lips and thought. 'Too risky. They might be monitoring my calls, or someone could have bugged this car.'

'What car?' Barbie asked.

I didn't answer though. 'Lose the uniforms, get off the ship and call me in an hour. Head for the middle of the island but use a rental car, not one of the limos.'

I got several okays in response and we were all about to disconnect when I thought of another question. 'Did Mrs Garland ever turn up?'

Mrs Garland

Mrs Garland was the wild card in the pack. She hadn't come back, which dumped on my belief that she had just wandered off for a little peace and quiet from the Tanners. I was actually feeling a little bad about being so dismissive about her disappearance now. Was she really in trouble?

There were so many moving parts for me to work out. Somewhere in the madness there was an international spy conspiracy going on and I held the thing they all wanted. On top of that there might be some kind of human trafficking organised crime ring operating who may or may not have Mrs Garland in their possession and the local police were after me and had my butler in custody. Why had Chief Rabat chosen to conduct my interview without legal counsel? He knew it would guarantee my release. Even if I was guilty of murder and he had evidence, it would have muddied the waters and given my defence real ammunition to use.

It was truly curious.

I needed to get myself some place where I could find a disguise. If Chief Rabat circulated my picture, it wouldn't be long before someone recognised me. That spurred a thought which got me out of the car.

What was in the boot of Emily's car?

The answer, I found, was a spy's treasure trove. I opened the lid, gasped and closed it again. Telling myself I should be thankful it wasn't filled with bodies, I checked the passing traffic wouldn't be able to see in and opened it again. A large holdall sat in line with the car down the left-hand side. It was open, last night's outfit lying on top, but the rest of the space was filled with guns and knives and, would you believe it, some kind of grenade. I didn't dare pick them up to read the label. There were other items that looked less likely to blow up though, I picked up weird looking goggles that I determined had to be some kind of night-vision device – there had to be half a dozen of those at least. There were binoculars, radios, things that looked like they were designed to adhere to something else by use of a magnet – I guessed they might be tracking devices though how to check where they were once deployed I had no idea, and, when I lifted other things out of the way, I found a case which contained a snap-together sniper rifle. Then there was a briefcase, the snaps of which I gingerly clicked, one eye closed and my face turned away half-terrified that it might explode. Inside were multiple passports, all with her face but each of them with a different name and different hair and each from a different Nation. Credit cards and wads of cash in more than a dozen currencies caught my eye. I had no idea how much money it came to, but it looked like a lot.

Emily wasn't a British spy, or if she was, or ever had been, she was one who had gone bad. Whoever resourced her, supplied some fun tools. Fun if your hobby was killing people, that is.

I got back into the car and checked the time. It was coming up on eleven o'clock. Barbie, Deepa and the others would be making their way to me but would be at least another hour I figured. I would give them a better location to find me when I decided where that might be. In the meantime, I was going to find someplace to change and hope I could wriggle my middle-aged bum into some of Emily's clothes.

Finding a place was easier than I could have hoped. Two miles further down the road from where I pulled off to call Deepa, I found a gas station. In the disabled cubicle of the ladies' toilet, I emptied Emily's holdall and picked through it. She liked skinny jeans. Well, none of them were going on me. I didn't even try. Instead, I sifted through to find another dress, something summery that might be looser and thus take in the extra girth I carried when compared to her.

Nothing worked. There was a summer dress, but it said size two on the label. I got it on, but I looked ridiculous; like an adult wearing their child's outfit. Harrumphing that she had to be so skinny, I stuffed the clothes away again and accepted that I was going to have to do what I didn't want to. I was going to have to disguise myself as a man again.

Stomping back out to the car and muttering under my breath about how stupid skinny women shouldn't be allowed, I threw her bag back into the car and picked up the bag I took from my hotel room at the last moment. When I grabbed it in haste last night, I hadn't realised it was the one I had stuffed the Sam Spade outfit into. It was only now, when I thought about needing to disguise myself that I realised what I had done.

It was both good, because it was an effective disguise, and bad, because I hated dressing up and had done way too much of it on this cruise.

Fifteen minutes later, I bumped into a pair of women my age as I let myself out of the ladies' toilets. 'This is the ladies,' one shouted after me.

With a smile on my face that the disguise worked, I bought water from a shop, got an odd look from the cashier, because the outfit only worked until a person took a proper look, and found a corner to sit in with a notepad and pen I found in the car. Before I got started, I needed to call the team.

Barbie's voice came on the line almost immediately. 'Hey, Patty. Are you done being cryptic? Can you tell us where you are now?' She sounded like she was in a great mood, brimming with excitement and raring to go.

'Sorry about all the mystery. When you get here, I will explain why it is necessary. I need you to keep going for a bit though. I stopped off to… well I'll explain that as well.' I gave her my location, heard her ask someone how far they were from it and got an ETA of about half an hour.

Barbie said they would be with me as soon as possible so I opened the notebook, chewed the end of the pen, and tried to organise my thoughts.

The first question I asked myself was, 'Where is Mrs Garland?' I said it out loud as I wrote it down. Was she the key to this or an absolute red herring? I wanted to believe that if the Algerians, or anyone else for that matter, were snatching women from Malta for prostitution or anything else in another country, they would move them really quickly. Take them, ship them. Bang, bang. That made sense because it minimised the risk. Unless… Unless… I couldn't quite put my finger on what my brain wanted to tell me.

I grabbed my phone and opened a search engine. Nora Garland was a rare enough name that she was the first and only hit. I learned to search people by their name from watching Jermaine and Barbie do it. Suddenly I had access to all manner of information about the missing grandmother. Her social profile wasn't very complete; it gave me the impression someone had helped her set it up, her daughter, or granddaughter maybe, but the interest hadn't been there, and no one maintained it now.

The relationship status said she was involved with someone and there were new pictures on her feed, arriving there because her daughter, Sarah Tanner, had tagged her.

Navigating to her photo albums, I found old pictures of her. When I found her wedding, I sat forward, her husband was wearing Royal Navy uniform and the scene behind them wasn't a churchyard in England; the hills were the same barren reddish, orangey-brown rock I saw everywhere

here. I turned my face to look out the window; the same thing was right outside if I looked beyond the carpark.

It wasn't hard evidence. In fact, it didn't tell me anything except that perhaps Nora Garland got married here. I made a mental note, checked to see if there was any other information of interest and went back out to her newsfeed page. There were the pictures Sarah tagged her in and her relationship status. I scanned it all again, decided there was nothing else to learn and closed it down.

Then I opened it again as quickly as I possibly could. I had to be wrong. My eyes had to be deceiving me, but they weren't. Frantically, I switched between apps, opening my messages to see the picture Gary Senior sent me yesterday.

In the last picture Sarah linked to her mother's social media profile, the family group were in Valetta. The ship was visible on the right-hand edge and the fortified walls of the city dominated the rest of the picture. I wasn't looking at any of that though. I wasn't even looking at how Gary Junior appeared to be scratching his groin. My eyes were drawn to the man who Nora was looking at.

He had on a garish stripy shirt. It was the same man who was in the back of the taxi when it left Quarry Wharf with her in it. He had been watching the family from the moment they left the ship. It made my blood run cold.

What did it tell me though? For starters, I was now sure that Nora had been taken. It was quite deliberate; the man in the stripy shirt picked her out and followed her. He was a poorly dressed, pudgy, white guy though, so if the human trafficking thing had any mileage in it, it felt out of place for him to be involved with the Algerians.

What role did the Algerians' play even? I thought they were involved in the trafficking but then Emily said they were a military unit. She lied, of course, I knew that already, but how much of what she said was lies, how much was guesswork and how much could actually be true?

I knew that human trafficking was happening because Chief Rabat admitted as much, telling me there was an undercover operation in process. Looking down, I had two pages of notes and absolutely no clue. I packed my things back into the bag and started back to the carpark. Barbie, Deepa and the others would be here in maybe another ten minutes, I might as well meet them outside.

'Oh, hello, could you help us?' asked a woman's voice as I got to the doors.

I swung my head around to find a woman about my age. Her accent was American Mid-West I thought, though I accepted that covered a lot of territory and there had to be regional differences between a person from Chicago and a person from Wisconsin. Her hair and clothes suggested she was a cattle farmer; all denims and a pair of cowboy boots.

I raised my eyebrows as she drew near. 'Hello.'

When I spoke, it caught her out. 'Oh, you're a woman. That is a different outfit for a lady to be wearing.' She looked me up and down, but not in a judgemental way, she appeared to just be assessing my wardrobe choices and wondering why I was dressed as a man, complete with wig and Bailey Fedora hat. 'Sorry,' she said, when she realised she was staring and not talking. 'You threw me there for a minute. Are you headin' outside?'

I pushed against the door my hand was already resting against. 'I am,' I replied as I led the way outside, hoping I could lose the woman but being polite.

'Well, my husband and I are having a little car trouble, you see. He sent me to see if I could find someone that might be able to help him. Well, I'm terrible with cars and engines and things like that, and truth be told my Wilber likes to think he knows what he is doing,' She glanced around. 'But he doesn't,' she added quietly like it was a secret no one was allowed to know. 'I spotted you and I thought, now there is a nice, tidy looking man. I bet he knows all about cars.'

We had crossed the road that ran directly in front of the gas station which wasn't so much a gas station as it was a truck stop, and we were into the carpark. 'I'm sorry,' I shrugged at her. 'I'm terrible with cars and engines and stuff like that,' choosing to repeat the phrase she herself had used because it summed up my knowledge base neatly.

'There's my Wilber,' she said, raising her arm to wave to him.

'I'm sorry,' I said again as I started to peel off toward Emily's car. 'I really can't be of any help.' I was about to turn around and wish her luck when she jabbed something into my right kidney, something hard like steel.

'You can help plenty by giving me the device, honey,' she hissed in my ear. She had a tight grip around my right bicep and was pulling me into the gun as she shoved it painfully into my back. Maintaining her grip, she turned me toward Wilber and her car. 'No tricks now, or I'll just shoot you and take the device.' Then she pushed me away to make distance between us, and it no longer looked like I was being taken under duress. When I cut my eyes to look at her, she sneered, 'What? You didn't think I recognised you? Some spy you would make; your picture is all over the planet. Especially here. Wanted for murder, eh?'

'I didn't do it,' my protest of denial came out automatically.

'I don't care, darlin',' she laughed. 'Now move, or I might forget my generous nature.'

I had no idea how they found me or even who they were, but the gun I got from the British agent was in the car along with the other weapons. I had disarmed myself because I didn't want to carry a gun. Right now though I was cursing that decision.

Wilber, which probably wasn't his name at all, waited for us to arrive. He had conveniently broken down at the far edge of the carpark, the bonnet raised and steam coming from it to make it look realistic. The carpark was filled with cars, lots of people stopping off for food and other provisions because it was midday, or thereabouts.

I reached the last of the parked cars and moved beyond them, driven on by the woman with the gun who was still right behind me. Wilber was twenty yards away. Would they shoot me once they had the device, or would they stuff me in the boot of their car and drive off? Could I pull the same trick with the two devices again? I still didn't know which was which so I could try it, but I was just as likely to give them exactly what they wanted.

A roar of an engine accelerating snapped my head around just in time to see Deepa Bhukari and Martin Baker in the front seat of a white Toyota with Barbie leaning through from the back seat. She was pointing and yelling something, but they weren't aiming for me.

The car hit the woman behind me just as she turned toward it and raised the gun in mute shock. She bounced up and over, coming to land in a heap a few yards from where she had been. A scream of rage from Wilbur came as no surprise but I still wasn't armed and had to bet that he would be.

Bullets hitting the white Toyota as it kept going confirmed my fear but as I looked around for the weapon the woman had been carrying, I could see no sign of it. The nearest cars were yards away, so I was unarmed, and I had no cover.

I was a sitting duck. Yet again.

As Wilbur stepped around his rigged broken-down car, he was too busy lining up his gun on me to pay attention to the car bearing down on him. Just like the woman, he saw it too late to evade it. The impact pitched him into the air and sent him flying, his gun spinning across the tarmac. The latest vehicular weapon was another white Toyota but this one had Lady Mary at the wheel. She slammed on the brakes, skidding to a halt as she fist-pumped the air.

I was sitting on the ground, my clothes probably getting dirty again, but where my nerves were frazzled and wanted to go for a lie down somewhere, Lady Mary was bouncing in her seat and looking about to see if there was anyone else she could run down. In the passenger seat of her car, Lieutenant Schneider looked terrified.

We were going to draw attention very soon; faces were already staring at us from the gas station where the unmistakable sound of gunfire would have been heard. Deepa's car was swinging around to come back, the news that both assailants were down having reached the driver.

People started to spill out of the cars. 'Are you alright, Mrs Fisher?' from Schneider, was followed very quickly by, 'Patty, are you hurt?' from Barbie and I had to raise my hands and beg for calm to make them stop.

'We are hip deep in it,' I said to get their attention focused. Pointing to the injured couple they had just run over, who were now groaning and trying to get up. 'Those two are probably spies though I couldn't tell you what nation they are from despite their convincing accents.'

'Wait a minute,' said Deepa, holding up her hands to get my attention. 'You just said spies? What are you mixed up in?'

'We need to leave,' I insisted, starting towards my car. 'They are not the only intelligence operatives I have faced today. We need to get out of here, get somewhere safe and then I will tell you what I know.'

'I'm driving,' shouted Lady Mary, already turning about to get back in her car.

'The heck you are!' argued Schneider. 'I'm all for a bit of action and adventure, but you drive like you have a death wish.'

She gave him a look that said he had to be nuts. 'Young man, you got into the car without asking me if I even have a license. I had three gins for breakfast. I'm stunned we are still alive – this is called living!' Then she whooped like a frat boy and punched a fist into the air.

'I'll take Lady Mary with me,' I volunteered, snagging her arm to drag her with me so we could avoid any further argument. Lady Mary opened her mouth to ask a question, but I got there first. 'No, Mary, I don't have any alcohol in the car.' She closed her mouth again with a disappointed look.

'Where do we meet?' asked Barbie.

They all looked confused when I told them.

Malta Royal Navy Base

The Royal Navy had long since left Malta, packing up in 1979 after Malta was granted independence from British rule in 1964. I learned all this with a quick internet search, but the information I wanted wasn't going to be found floating in the ether. However, it might be possible to get it from the Royal Navy Museum located on the site of the original guardroom at the entrance to the dockyard. It was right back in Valetta though, a place where a concentration of police were looking for me and somewhere I should most certainly be trying to avoid.

According to Lady Mary, I had no hope of getting back to the ship without being arrested. The local police had formed a cordon and were checking everyone coming onto the dock in the hope they could catch me, or otherwise prevent me from escaping to the ship. Her news didn't fill me with joy, though she seemed energised by all that was happening.

We found the Royal Navy Museum easily enough by the simple expedient of following the signposts, though we had a reasonably good idea where it was anyway. My concern was always that I might be spotted, but Chief Rabat had hedged his bets by sending a force to the dock to catch me there. It left the streets largely devoid of squad cars and we saw not one police uniform as we drove around Valetta.

The museum was a small place, barely bigger than my old four-bedroom detached house in England, though there was a warehouse at the back which looked to be part of it. The building itself appeared to be two hundred years old or more. It reminded me of Chatham Dockyard, a tourist attraction not far from my home town. I visited there once a few years ago with my man-eating, husband stealing ex-friend, Maggie. They had an open day and she wanted to ogle the guys in their uniforms. The buildings there were much the same as this one; built from red brick with a door in the centre and two sets of large sash windows either side.

The signs outside were modern, the lines for the parking bays in the carpark newly painted. The car park was empty though, not a car in it, which made me wonder if it was even open. Where had the staff parked?

Angling into a space at the front of the carpark and near to the museum building, I saw a shadow move behind a window; someone was inside. Baker and Schneider, driving the other two cars, parked either side of me, the eight of us spilling out.

Everyone looked ready to head inside, but not without some expectant looks in my direction because I promised to tell them what was going on. Mentally, I thanked them for being trusting enough to come with me this far despite having no clue what I was dragging them into.

I sat on the boot lid of Emily's car as the team gathered around me and I held up the little black data storage device.

Barbie said, 'It's a thumb drive.'

'What's a thumb drive?' asked Lady Mary.

'You can carry computer files around on it,' supplied Hideki. 'They save a person needing to carry a computer a lot of the time.'

Lady Mary groaned, 'Wretched things.'

She looked like she had more to say on the subject but I cut her off, looking at the four members of the security team when I said, 'Do you remember the man in the paraglider who landed on the ship when it left Athens?' They all nodded. 'He gave me this.' My statement got seven sets of raised eyebrows. 'I don't want to tell you more than you need to know, but he is British Intelligence and he was hurt.'

'Yes, we found blood where he landed,' remembered Schneider.

'That's right. Well, he came all the way to Malta with us, and he asked me to take this to his contact because he believed he was being pursued by operatives from other countries.'

'What's on it?' Barbie asked.

I gave my honest answer with a shrug. 'I don't know for sure. He said it was a weapon of some kind. Or blueprints for a weapon. Whatever it is, the boffins who came up with it were all killed.' Barbie drew in a quick breath of shock. 'And there are a number of people still after it.'

Baker took a turn to ask a question, 'Is that why there were two bodies found in your hotel room last night?'

I nodded, 'Yes, but I don't think they were after the weapon.'

Hideki frowned. 'How come?'

'Because they made no attempt to get it. They didn't even ask about it, which is the first question I get from everyone else involved. They were shot by a woman who claimed to also be British Intelligence, but she wasn't. She baited me into leading her to the British spy's contact in Mdina because the data on this thing cannot be accessed without a decryption device. She shot him, tried to steal the decryptor and the data storage device and I barely got away.'

'What happened?' Lady Mary's voice was a soft murmur, everyone listening intently to my story.

'Another agency arrived, there was a shootout, I escaped. She then got in a car which exploded.'

'The terrorist bomb we heard about on the radio,' said Pippin, putting two and two together. 'That was you.'

'It wasn't me, thankfully. I mean, I didn't set the bomb and I didn't get blown up, but I was there. Anyway, I still have the data device containing the weapon and half the spies on the planet will gladly kill to get their hands on it. You saw that for yourselves at the gas station. Those two had American accents but they might have been from anywhere.' I took a moment to make eye contact with each single person in the group. 'I tell you that because I need you to understand the stakes. They have never been higher. This isn't a deranged man out for vengeance, it isn't a woman who believes her husband is cheating on her or even rival gangs arguing over Al Capone's shoes; these are professional killers and my advice to you, is to go back to the ship and stay there until it sails tomorrow.'

'What will you do, Patty?' asked Barbie quietly.

I fixed a hard look on my face, wanting to look determined even though I felt terrified. 'I have to finish this.'

'Then we are with you,' Baker said, speaking for the whole group, but they all agreed with him.

Even Lady Mary, who said, 'There had better be some good gin waiting at the end of this.'

Hideki nodded his head at the museum. 'So what are we doing here?'

It was the perfect question for someone to ask. 'We are here, because the spy thing isn't the only problem we have.' Then, as they hit me with a fresh salvo of wide eyes and raised eyebrows, I told them about Mrs Garland, the Algerians, Chief Rabat and the possible human trafficking ring I had stumbled onto.

When I finished, our little huddle were almost touching shoulders, the complexity and danger of the problem drawing them ever closer as I tried to lay it out.

'Hello,' said a friendly man's voice at a volume loud enough to scare the pants off everyone. We fell about, clutching our hearts and gasping for breath. 'I'm sorry, did I make you jump?' he asked.

I turned to find a man in his sixties, a huge, grey, handlebar mustache dominating his face beneath wire-rimmed spectacles. He wore a tweed jacket with leather elbow patches over a white cotton shirt. A navy-blue tie, pinned in place by a gold crest told me he was retired Royal Navy. I held up a finger to beg for a moment.

'You've been out here a while, you see?' the man said. 'I don't mind you using the carpark for your little meeting. It's not like I get many visitors, but I just wanted to know if you were planning to come in because if not, I was going to pop off for a little bit of lunch at the local pub.'

'We're coming in,' I managed, straightening up now that my heart had gone back to pumping blood. 'Actually, I have some research I need to do and you look like exactly the person to help me.'

'Research?' the man repeated. His eyes were twinkling like I had just offered him a gift. 'I'm ready when you are.' We all followed him to the building, there being no reason for anyone to stay outside. At the door, the gentleman introduced himself as Commodore (retired) Dougal Brown. Inside, there was an assistant in the form of a young Maltese woman called Angelica. 'Come in, come in,' the commodore beckoned. 'We won't worry about charging you for entrance, not considering who you are.'

'You recognise me?' I asked.

'Oh, yes,' he replied, still leading us further into the museum. 'The disguise is a good idea though; your picture is all over the news at the moment.'

'You're not calling the police?' Deepa confirmed.

'Heavens, no, dear.' He looked at Deepa as if the idea was ridiculous. 'Those horrors gave me a speeding ticket last year. They can go whistle. Now then, dear lady, what it is you want to find out?'

I probably should have led with the question I was about to ask because if his archive didn't have this kind of information, there was no point in us hanging around any longer. 'Do you have records of weddings that took place at the Naval base?'

The question surprised him, but he didn't query why I wanted to know. 'Yes, dear. I think we can find that. Follow me please.'

In a back room of the building, the commodore showed us large drawers filled with photographs and shelf upon shelf of ledgers.

'Wow,' said Barbie. 'This looks like it might take a while. What are we looking for again?'

'Anything to do with Nora Garland,' I supplied, speaking to the entire group and the commodore. 'She won't have been Nora Garland until she got married so we are looking for her husband really. He was in Navy whites for their wedding.'

'Do you have a picture?' the commodore asked.

I said, 'It's on her social media profile,'

Barbie was fastest to get her phone out, saying, 'I'm on it,' then spelling out the name to herself as she typed it in. 'Was it in a particular album?' she asked. I skewed my lips to show I couldn't say. I wasn't sure how a person discerned one album from the next. I could just about find the albums; anything more was like doing magic.

Barbie found it in about eight seconds.

'Oh, yes,' said the commodore, taking off one pair of glasses and putting on another pair as he squinted at the picture on her phone. 'I recognise exactly where that picture was taken. Do you know what year it was?'

Barbie looked at me. I looked at her and then tried to do some math. 'Her daughter is late thirties or maybe forty, so Nora has to be early sixties unless Sarah was not her first child or if she came late. From the pictures...'

'She's seventy-one,' said Barbie, holding up her phone to show us a picture of a big birthday bash. The cake in the photo bore two candles in the shape of a seven and a zero and the date the picture was uploaded to her social media profile was fourteen months ago.

'She looks about twenty in her wedding photo so we can narrow the search down to a few years. Let's go back fifty years and search that year and the two years either side of it.'

Dutifully, the commodore picked his way along the shelves to the section he wanted and started taking down ledgers. 'These are from the church archives. They were moved here when they knocked it down to build hotels.'

'That's terrible,' I commented. It horrified me that old buildings were bulldozed to make way for new, money no doubt the driver behind it.

'Well, it had a great position overlooking the sea, but they took it apart brick by brick and moved it half a mile inland. They also bought the land for a substantial sum, so I think the church did okay out of it.' He passed he ledgers to Baker, Bhukari, Pippin, Hideki and Schneider, who carried them to a table. 'Her husband was a flyer you know.'

I gave him a raised eyebrow.

'A navy pilot,' he explained. 'You can tell by the emblem on his uniform. They were called the parrots. I don't think they liked the nickname, but it stuck, and, in the end, they used it as their emblem.'

'Patty,' Barbie called to get my attention as the team started going through the ledgers. 'She's not here with a husband or anything is she? It's just her family, you said.'

'Yes, that's right.'

'Well, her relationship status shows that it was changed yesterday. She changed it from not in a relationship, to in a relationship at quarter past two yesterday afternoon.'

My mouth dropped open. 'Can someone else do that for her? I mean, can someone else get into her feed and update her information?'

'Yes,' Barbie admitted. 'But only if they have her password. Why would anyone want to do that?'

I didn't have an answer for her. Or rather I did, but it was one that didn't fit. If no one else had amended her profile, then she had to have been the one to do it.

Barbie came to stand next to me so I could see her phone as well. 'It looks like her husband died just after her birthday a year ago. There are lots of posts by her up until then, but nothing since. The only updates are linked pictures from her daughter. Until yesterday, but there's nothing written. Just the change to her status.'

Did that mean something? It brought into question everything I thought I believed about Mrs Garland and what might have happened to her.

'Found it,' announced Deepa, raising her hand to get our attention. 'Marriage of Second Lieutenant James Garland to Nora Montrose on July 8th, 1958. Marriage took place at Our Lady of Grace Catholic church in Valetta.'

I came to join her, sliding between Pippin and Schneider to get a look at the page. It was a record of the marriage but nothing more. The bride and groom had signed beneath their names as had the two witnesses. I borrowed Barbie's phone to take a picture in case we needed the information later, but it hadn't taken me in the direction I hoped it might.

Barbie touched my arm. 'Patty, can I see the data storage device?'

'Um, yeah, sure.' My brain was whirling with questions, each of which was taking me down a dead end when I tried to answer them. I handed over both black data drives and paid no attention to what Barbie was doing until she said a bad word.

I think we all turned in her direction, but only I knew what was happening. Barbie had spotted a computer in the corner and plugged one of the drives into it. Smoke was pouring out already as it sparked and fizzed. I dashed across the room to yank the device free.

'I wanted to see what was on it that was so important,' she admitted guiltily. Pippin nudged her out of the way as he arrived carrying a fire extinguisher. A few blasts of dry powder killed the fire and also finished off the computer.

'I should have told you about this bit. The police did the same thing at the station. I don't know what is on here or what it is supposed to do, but if you plug it into a standard computer, the computer catches fire.'

Barbie's face was blushing red and horrified. 'Right. Good tip to remember.' She made eye contact with the commodore. 'Sorry,' she said with an embarrassed look.

I held the slightly warm data drive in my right hand. I now knew which was the real one. This time I zipped it carefully into a separate compartment of my handbag and dropped the dummy one into the main well in the middle. If I could remember which one was where now, I would be able to hand someone the wrong one if I wanted to.

'I have a question,' Lady Mary announced, taking advantage of a lull in the conversation as she looped her arm through the commodore's. 'They used to serve tots of rum on board the Royal Navy ships, did they not?'

'Yes, indeed,' the commodore replied happily. 'That practice kept going until July 31st, 1970 when it was no longer deemed in keeping with modern times or safety practices.'

'How much is a tot?' she asked.

'Ah, good question, my dear. A tot, which one might think is quite a small amount, is, in fact, a quarter of a pint.'

'Was it strong stuff?' Lady Mary was all about the alcohol.

'Goodness, yes. Traditionally, navy warships served Pussar's rum which was, and still is, forty-two percent proof. It was given neat, and it was not untypical for sailors, who had performed a special task or earned some form of reward, to receive such a reward as an additional tot.'

'Half a pint of rum,' murmured Lady Mary, a dreamy look on her face. 'Was there a particular time of the day when the rum was served?'

'Actually, there was. Because the ship had to be manned twenty-four hours a day, different watches would get their tot at different times. I was always fond of the one o'clock ration. It set me up for the afternoon I found.'

Lady Mary grinned at him. Then showed him her watch. She had walked him into a trap. 'Shall we?' she asked, a cheeky grin on her face.

'Oh, um, well, yes, perhaps we should.' The commodore toddled away to find a decanter and I caught Lady Mary's eye and shook my head to show my despair.

I got a fake confused look in response. 'A person could die of thirst here, Patricia.'

I let it go, there were more important things to deal with. Sirens in the distance brought my head up, Baker and I locking eyes across the table. 'You don't think...' he asked.

'We should check,' I replied. He was asking if they were heading in our direction and somehow knew we were here. Who would have called them though?

Baker came running back into the room. 'There's a pair of squad cars heading this way. I locked the front door, but we need a new way out of here.'

'Dammit,' said Lady Mary as the commodore came back through the door with a decanter and glasses on an ornate tray in his hands. She had exactly what she wanted and no time to savour it.

'How would they know we were here?' asked Hideki.

We all looked at the commodore. 'Goodness, no,' he objected, our stares sufficient without needing to vocalise the question.

I nodded my head sadly. 'Where's your assistant?' His eyes went wide as he saw the truth of it. She had called them, but we had no time to dwell on it. 'There's nothing more here for us. Commodore, is there a back way out.'

'Yes, yes,' he blurted, dancing about as he looked around for somewhere to put the tray of rum down. Schneider took it from him and dumped it on top of the ledgers. Then we followed the commodore as he raced out of the room.

Race was a comparative word though. His pace was more of an amble and the sirens were getting really loud now. He paused and stood to one side, pointing onwards as he shouted, 'The door is just ahead. I'll get them to come inside so you can get back around the front to your cars. Just watch from the corner, give me a ten count once they are inside and don't look back. Good luck to you all,' he called as we departed.

Schneider got to the corner first, peered carefully around it as the rest of us flattened ourselves to the wall, then gave come-on motions when the coast was clear. We all ran to the cars, bent over at the waist to keep low in case anyone looked out of a window.

'Where are we going now?' whispered Barbie as we neared the cars.

I shot a lord-only-knows-look. 'Let's just get out of Valetta and regroup.' Then I had a better idea. 'Let's go to the market.'

'Which market?'

'The one right outside the city wall. It's there every day, or so it claims in my travel guide. There'll be lots of people so we can hide in plain sight. Let's go there and then make a plan. Okay?'

She shrugged an okay at me and we all dived into our respective cars.

I had an idea forming.

Valetta Market

I was right about the market being busy. There were hundreds of stalls crammed into a tight space outside the ancient entrance to the walled city. Overhead there were canvas sheets to keep the sun off the traders, the effect for us one of safety as we were invisible from all directions.

Crowded into a huddle behind a stall which sold kebabs, I tried to explain what I thought might be happening. 'I think we accidentally stumbled across a human trafficking ring operating in Malta. When I had the argument with the Tanners on Quarry Wharf, we were overheard and that set them after me; they wanted to know what I knew.'

'What do you know?' asked Lady Mary.

I gave her the honest answer, 'Nothing. I think though, that we need to find out something so we can draw them in. I think the Algerian men that came to my hotel room are the ones who took Alistair. I propose to contact them and set up an exchange.'

'What will we exchange?' asked Barbie.

'Nothing.' Everyone stared at me. 'We don't have anything. So we either have to come up with a clever bluff, or find something they will want more than Alistair.'

'How long will they hold him before...' Deepa started the sentence but didn't want to finish it.

'Before they kill him?' I finished it for her. 'I don't know, but probably not long. My assumption is they took him to force me to talk but the men they left to interrogate me were killed before they got a chance to ask any questions.'

'Why wouldn't they just take you?' asked Schneider.

It was really good question and one which had been bugging me since last night. 'I think they were told not to. I think this has something to do with who I am and about not drawing extra attention to themselves. Kill me and too many people might look their way. If they are, in fact, involved in human trafficking, they want as little scrutiny as possible.'

'They also want protection from local interference,' added Baker.

Deepa agreed, 'That's right. There has to be someone inside the local police who is helping them.'

'Yes,' I nodded. 'That is my assumption also. The police chief I met was very secretive, I think he suspects people within his organisation. He made sure the interview wasn't recorded. I thought he was trying to trap me, but now I wonder if maybe he was trying to make sure no one else could listen to the interview afterward.'

'So the police are involved,' said Barbie, 'Which means if we work out who has the captain, we can't go to them for help.'

I shook my head. 'No, we can't. I have an idea about that though.'

'Goodness, Patricia sweetie. Tell us what it is,' insisted Lady Mary.

I shook my head again. 'Not yet. First I want to work out what happened to Mrs Garland.'

'We don't have much to go on,' complained Deepa. 'We know she got married here and we know she went to Sliema in a taxi with a man in a stripy shirt yesterday.'

I had to contest her point, 'We also know where she got out of that taxi and we know who signed as her witnesses.'

'That doesn't seem like much to go on,' argued Baker.

I agreed with them, 'That's because it isn't.' They were right, there was no sense in arguing but I had no intention of being defeated. I wanted Alistair back and though this wasn't really part of it, it went a long way to proving my theories, and that, ultimately, would allow me to close the net on everyone involved.

Barbie huffed out a breath, a sort of half laugh that got everyone's attention. 'I was just thinking that this is usually the point when Patty gives each of us tasks to do that seem to make no sense until we get them done and she solves the case.' She and everyone else turned their eyes my way and looked at me expectantly.

I pursed my lips and looked at the sky. I found myself flipping a mental coin because there were so many elements to control. Finally, I said, 'It will be dark soon. This is what we need to do.'

Help Needed

I was sure of two things. The first was that in order to get Alistair back safely, I was going to have to put people at risk. The second was that we couldn't hope to succeed without some additional help. I had an idea for the second problem though.

There were a lot of things to do quite quickly, most of them happening all at once. I sent Lady Mary with Lieutenant Schneider to return to the ship. I could have just made a phone call but person to person was more likely to yield the result we needed, especially given the nature of my request.

With them gone, I dispatched Deepa Bhukari and Martin Baker to go shopping. No one was looking for them so they could walk freely into Valetta to find an upmarket boutique. The simple instruction for Deepa was to buy something slutty for her and Barbie. She knew Barbie's size; it was quite easy to remember after all. Shortly, the pair of them would be doing their best to attract some very particular attention.

In the meantime, I had her and Pippin and Hideki all looking through social media for something very specific. And while they did that, I tried to solve the missing Mrs Garland case head on. I had a little inkling about where Mrs Garland might have gone and why. There were clues pointing toward it though they were all very minor and could equally mean nothing. I chose to follow them though and hope for the best.

Malta had an accessible online directory of enquiries just like everywhere else. The name James Barnstable was listed as a witness on her wedding certificate. The other witness's name was Elsa Barnstable, making them a married couple. The best man in the photographs, James Barnstable, was also in Royal Navy whites and bore the same parrot emblem on his uniform. Looking through the wedding pictures earlier, there was one photograph that got my attention more than any other. It told a story. A story which could be interpreted different ways, depending on a person's point of view and life experiences. I hadn't told anyone what I thought it might mean yet, but I was going to try to find out now.

The directory of enquiries gave me three James Barnstables to pick from. It told me nothing more about them, so I started at the top and made a call.

The first call was answered but it was a young man at the other end. I asked if he knew a person by the name Nora Garland and listened for his response. When he said no, I got no sense that he was lying, so I thanked him and moved on.

The second call went through to another man who sounded too young to be the man I wanted. He wasn't James Barnstable though, he was his son, innocently offering to get his dad for me. When a man who sounded significantly older said, 'Hello?' I allowed a ray of hope to sneak in.

'Good evening. I am hoping to speak to Nora Garland. Can you put her on the phone, please?' I got silence. 'Her family are very worried about her. They don't know where she is.'

More silence. Just when I thought I was going to have to lean on him a little harder, he said, 'I'm sorry, I think you have the wrong number. I don't know a Nora Garland.'

'Wasn't she the wife of one of your best friends?' I prompted quickly, worried he might hang up.

'You have the wrong number,' he repeated and then the line when dead.

I tapped my phone on my chin in thought. I couldn't be certain he was lying. Or that Nora was there if he was lying. I couldn't even be certain I had the right James Barnstable, so I tried the third number and got a West Indian accent delivered in a rumbling bass. I pretended to be calling about insurance, confirmed I was indeed talking to James Barnstable and got off the phone. It was getting late and there was a lot to do yet, so I put the issue of Nora Garland to one side for a while. I believed I had it worked out, but there was nothing I could do about it tonight.

With that task complete, I blew out a nervous breath, bit my lip and took a selfie. The selfie had the main entrance to Valetta in the near background, a clear marker so they would know where I was and the slim black mass data storage device was in my left hand. Then I posted it to my social media profile and wrote a note to go with it:

'I still have what you want. I don't want it. I want no further part of the violence and will happily hand it over to the first ones to come for it. I will be here tomorrow morning at nine o'clock and will provide instructions to retrieve it.'

The spies and government agents would come. They had to be monitoring such things; I knew I was. Justin could easily pop up in disguise again at any moment, but I no longer cared. I was going to give them the dummy device and wave them all goodbye. The ship was due to sail at noon tomorrow. I could give them the device and leave them all behind provided tonight's crazy plan brought Alistair back to me. I hadn't told anyone on my team about my plan for the device with the super-weapon on it. Were I to do so, they would simply try to come with me tomorrow for the exchange. I had an idea about how to give it to the competing agencies attempting to retrieve it without giving them a chance to see me, but just like Nora Garland it could wait for now; there were more pressing issues.

One element I was yet to tackle was that of my missing butler, Jermaine. To my knowledge, he languished still in a Maltese cell, waiting for the lawyer, O'Donnell, to arrange his release. Would I even leave Malta if he was still behind bars?

I pushed it to one side as Barbie called to get my attention. 'I think you were right, Patty,' I wanted to make a clever quip about her statement being utterly redundant because of course I was. I could never allow myself to display that kind of arrogance though, not even in jest as proposed, so I went to see what she had found. 'He's there in the pictures.' On her phone, Barbie had a photograph of a man in his late thirties. She held the phone in her right hand, and, in her left, she had Hideki's phone in which was displayed the picture from Nora's social media page; the one of the family group in Valetta with the man watching them.

It was the same man. When I first saw the picture, I took the man in the stripy shirt to be stalking them. Or to be watching them because he had a criminal plan in mind. Seeing him in the back of a taxi with his arm around Mrs Garland strengthened that impression. Now I knew who he was.

'That's it then,' I said.

Barbie nodded in agreement. 'I think it is.'

Pippin asked, 'Do we tell them? The Tanners, I mean. Do we let them know?'

I shook my head. 'We can't. Not yet, at least. Dealing with them will become a distraction when we can ill afford one. We will let them know once we have Alistair back and have wrapped that business up. The Tanners can wait.' I wasn't being cruel, I felt certain the daughter, Sarah, was in anguish regarding the whereabouts of her mother. It wasn't pressing though. She would survive a sleepless night, but someone else might not survive tonight if I wasn't on the ball.

With the issue of Mrs Garland's whereabouts almost certainly deduced, and the stupid spies given a time and a place to come for me, I felt I could focus on the human trafficking problem and get Alistair back.

My phone rang. I looked down at it, hoping it would be the call I needed: it was. And so I hoped I would get the news I wanted: I didn't. Or rather, I did, but not quite as I expected.

'Lieutenant Schneider, have you been successful?'

His voice came on the line, 'Mrs Fisher, can I put you on speaker phone?'

'Of course.' I took the phone away from my ear and held it out so Barbie and the others could crowd around it. 'What have you got for us.'

A new voice answered, but it was one which I recognised. 'Mrs Fisher, this is Commander Yusef, the ship's deputy captain.' He really didn't need to introduce himself and certainly didn't need to say what his position was. I understood why he did it when he spoke again. 'I have a person to introduce you to. Interpol dispatched an agent at our request. He arrived an hour ago.'

'Good evening, Mrs Fisher,' a new voice said, 'This is Manos Vardalos. I understand that you may have a lead on the human trafficking going on in Malta.'

It was a very open statement and had no question attached to it even though one was implied. I replied anyway, 'I believe that to be the case. I think they have people within the Maltese police force who are protecting them or allowing them to operate without interference.'

'That would be typical,' he replied. 'Organised crime perpetuates itself by paying off key persons of influence. It ensures they look the other way or know when not to send patrols to a certain area.'

Commander Yusef's voice came back, 'Lieutenant Baker tells me you will need our help tonight.'

'That's right, Commander. I'm glad Interpol are represented actually. That will make what I want to do far less complex.'

'How's that?' asked Manos.

I closed my eyes for a moment, picturing all that needed to happen and in what order. 'Interpol have no powers as police, correct?'

'In a sense, yes,' Manos's answer was guarded like he didn't like the suggestion he lacked authority or power.

'But you are able to coordinate other forces, correct? And supervise the arrest of criminals regardless of nationality and allegiance.' I waited for his answer.'

Again, it came with a degree of defence in it. 'Yes, that is essentially correct.'

'Good. Well, gentlemen, this is what I need you do to.' I gave them the details of my plan. At least, I gave them the details I needed them to know. I didn't tell them the whole thing because they never would have agreed to it if I had. They knew enough to believe there was a high degree of probability that we would succeed. We would get the captain back, which is why the ship's security force would help. And we were likely to crack a human trafficking ring which is why Interpol was interested.

By the time I finished, they had both agreed to give me the help I needed, and I breathed a huge sigh of relief, both mentally and physically, a sense of something akin to exhaustion stealing over me. Lieutenant Schneider said he was on his way back with Lady Mary and would see us soon.

Just as he ended the call Deepa returned. 'Will this do?' she asked.

The Snatch

Now we were into the part of the plan that required us to get lucky. We were going fishing. I wanted to catch some Algerians, and my bait of choice was a tasty bit of drunk young woman.

Deepa and Barbie were sober, of course, but looking inebriated would make them look more vulnerable which was what we wanted. Deepa returned wearing a short dress that revealed more thigh than I had ever dared to bare in my life and did a very good job of forcing her boobs up and out. To go with it, she had thigh-length boots, the type where the leg part is more like a sheer sock than anything else and did a great job of showing off the shape beneath. The chaps were trying quite hard not to notice how her chest moved every time she breathed, a problem that doubled when Barbie appeared in the complimenting outfit Deepa picked out for her.

'I look like a hooker,' Barbie said as she did her best to tug her skirt down a half centimetre, so it covered the bottom curve of her cheeks. 'Seriously, Deepa, who is this outfit designed for?'

'I like it,' said Hideki, smiling at his girlfriend and then withering under the power of her glare.

'Can we get on with it?' Barbie asked. 'I'm getting quite nervous and being basically naked in the street isn't helping.'

Deepa looped an arm though hers, poured out the contents of a cheap champagne bottle and refilled it with water. 'I'm ready.'

Barbie muttered some choice words, but Baker and Schneider stepped in to reassure her. 'We'll never be more than a few yards from you. They will be focused on you and won't see us until it is too late. You both have tasers, yes?' Baker asked.

Both girls opened their handbags and showed they not only had them, but they were fully charged. Schneider found them in the treasure trove of gear in the boot of Emily's car. They also took handguns in case they needed to use them; they could be ditched far more easily than their own issued sidearms.

'What do we do?' asked Lady Mary.

'Mostly we stay out of sight until this part of the plan is done. There's not much we can do until we catch our fish.'

There was nothing left to say, so Deepa and Barbie set off, swaying and staggering every now and then, swigging from the champagne bottle filled with water and getting lots of attention and comments from men of all ages and races. Through it all, they kept going toward their destination: Quarry Wharf.

They dealt with the wolf whistles and lewd remarks as if they were women out to find men and were inebriated enough to not be too picky about who the man was. They were laughing and making comments in return but ultimately continuing on in a straight line. Twenty yards back, Baker and Pippin meandered along paying them no attention. They weren't looking at the girls at all, they were looking at the men looking at the girls. And that's what Schneider was doing on the opposite side of the road, keeping to the shadows without making it look like he was doing so deliberately. Every now and then he would pop into a shop so his passage through the town looked natural.

I was the odd one out in my stupid Sam Spade suit and hat, but I looked like a man until one looked closely, so Lady Mary and I were walking arm in arm as if we were a couple. I got one or two looks, but the eyes never lingered; it was evening in a holiday destination: there were far weirder things to look at than me.

Quarry Wharf was a shot in the dark in that I had no idea if the Algerians had been there yesterday by pure coincidence, or because they were there all the time. The route from Valetta's main entrance, where the market was located, to Quarry Wharf near the water, took them right through town, so if the Algerians were operating here, they were likely to have seen them. They presented as two attractive women with no attached male protection, which meant they would be perceived as most likely here by themselves and could be snatched and taken out of the country before they were reported as missing.

By the time we reached Quarry Wharf, we knew they had been clocked; a man was following them and trying to catch up. He was by himself, he looked sober, and he appeared to be the same racial heritage as the two Algerian men I briefly met.

He wasn't very vigilant though. Baker and Pippin were closing the gap on him and Schneider wasn't far behind either. We were all close enough, in fact, that we heard his words when he spoke. 'Ladies, does either one of you have a light?'

His seemingly harmless question could be considered just that if one hadn't just watched him follow them for over one hundred yards and pass thirty people, some of whom were smoking. The question then was intended solely to get them to stop. As they did, Baker, Pippin, and Schneider all stepped into shadows and waited.

I kept going, Lady Mary with me, our arms interlinked. If this was it, it might happen fast, and I wanted to be close by. The one man we could see wasn't going to take them; he was just there to spring the trap. I ran it through in my head: identify a target or, in this case, targets, send a message ahead and get the targets to stop. Then you would want a car or a van and an overwhelming number of additional men to grab the targets and take them.

A van appeared. It was coming toward us and would reach the girls and the man first. The girls sensed that this might be it, so they didn't have a light to offer him but were making conversation anyway; laughing and being tactile.

As the van neared, Schneider and the other guys moved. Lady Mary and I hung back, getting close to a wall so we were less visible. We were not going to be part of this bit; the middle-aged women weren't helpless, but trained security staff with weapons would operate more slickly without us in the way.

With twenty yards to go, the van shot forward, the driver inside stomping hard on the accelerator to create a shock effect that would stun their targets. He hit the brakes with five yards to go and skidded the rest of the way to stop right by them. The back doors flew open, visible either side of the van as we looked at the front and the sound of boots hitting the street told everyone it was go time.

There were four of them, plus the spotter in the street already talking to the girls, plus the driver if needed, though I was certain his instruction would be to stay in the van unless called for. Clearly, they had done this many times before because there was no chatter, no need to ask what any one of them needed to do next. They were slick and practiced.

They didn't get to do any of it of course. The spotter went down first. Deepa hitting him over the head with the champagne bottle full of water. It didn't even break which must have been like getting smacked with a bowling pin. Her move surprised the two Algerians on their side of the van, but not as much as the surprise they got when both girls shot tasers into their chests.

The other two Algerians had gone around the far side of the van. Presumably to cut off the girls' escape if they tried to run. They got to the front of the vehicle where Baker and Schneider stuck guns in their faces. Their hands went up instinctively and Hideki shot them both using a taser in each hand.

The only man left was the driver whose eyes were wide with shock and fear. He could have escaped if he had reacted swiftly enough and hit the gas, but his chance was gone the moment Pippin leaned in from the girls' side and pointed his gun at him. His arms went up in surrender and another part of the plan was complete.

I was stunned at how well it had gone.

'Can I get changed now?' asked Barbie.

The Lure

'They are useless to you,' scoffed one of the Algerians. I couldn't tell if he was the leader of their group or just the one that liked to talk but he wouldn't shut up. 'We use codes, so you can try to read our messages all day, but you will get nothing from them.'

We took their weapons and their phones the moment we had them. Then, while they were still twitching from the effects of being tasered, we used plastic cuffs to bind them and loaded them into their own van. Amazingly no one had seen us, but I worried they might be expected to report back so we took the van and drove it to the safe place I had picked out.

Well, I say I picked it out. What I did was ask my foursome of security crew where we could go that belonged to Purple Star Cruise Lines but wasn't the ship. It was Baker that suggested the warehouse they use for storing supplies and food and repair equipment and all manner of other items a massive cruise line needed to resupply and keep its ships in top condition.

It was manned twenty-four hours and with a ship in dock it ought to have been a hive of activity. Commander Yusef had made sure it was emptied of its usual manpower and left open for us to use though. So that's where we were, with our captive Algerians and their phones.

I didn't want to read their messages though. That was a task Interpol could perform at their leisure once they had people in custody. No, I wanted to know where the phones had been, and I knew my super tech-savvy friends could do stuff like that. Apparently, modern phones log where you are every second of the day. I knew there were functions like this because whenever I opened my social media profile it asked me if I wanted to check in. I had pressed it once or twice to see what it would do, only to find it knew precisely where I was and would report it to the world.

Hideki, Barbie, Deepa, and all the others had a phone each while Lady Mary and I, the dinosaurs that we are, watched on as the mysterious art of phone fiddling went on. The six of them were in a huddle, discussing what they were looking at and I tried to be patient but the annoying Algerian with the big mouth wouldn't shut up.

'You ought to be running,' he laughed. 'The longer you leave it to escape, the more likely it is that you will be caught. The guys will have it easy, of course, we'll just shoot them. Shoot them and take their bodies out to sea for the fishes. The women, well, let's just say you won't be in Malta for very much longer and you will probably wish you were one of the men.'

'I think we have it,' announced Schneider. He split away from the group to come to me, but the others came with him. Holding up one of the phones, he said, 'All of the phones spent a significant amount of time at this address. On the map it looks like a big storeroom but it backs onto the waterfront so they could easily run boats up to it and take people out that way, meeting a larger boat out to sea somewhere.'

'Okay,' I nodded. It was time to set in motion the part where we either won or all got killed. 'Let's send the message.'

Everyone sent a message to the primary contact in the phone. The one used most often which I guessed was the boss man or a lieutenant of his. The message was simple. 'We have your men at the Purple Star Cruise Lines Warehouse on the Western dock in Valetta. We want to exchange.'

The message was deliberately ambiguous. I didn't want them to bring Alistair. If they did that they would come in with a gun to his head and immediately have the upper hand. I wanted them to come without him.

They would come in numbers and armed to the teeth, but not until they had called whoever they were dealing with in the police to make sure they weren't walking into some kind of a trap. The police would know it was happening and make sure none of their people were anywhere near our location.

Which is why I called Chief Rabat. His number was easy to get; it was on the internet under local police. Not his personal mobile of course, but a number for a contact at the station who could then patch me through to him.

'Mrs Fisher?' he asked.

'Yes. Good evening Chief Rabat.'

'Are you calling to turn yourself in?'

'Hardly. I wasn't sure you would catch the real killers or solve the case of what happened to the man in Club Rhumbla so I decided to solve it all for myself.'

I heard him choking at the other end. 'Really, Mrs Fisher. So you think you know everything now, do you? What is it you propose to do with the information?'

'I propose to get back on my ship and sail home as planned. I need you to arrest a few men though. I am in the process of busting the human trafficking operation here. I have several of the men responsible in custody already and expect to have many more soon. If you want to claim the bust for yourself, you can have it; I just want to go home. You need to come to the Western dock in Valetta harbour. There is a Purple Star Cruise Lines warehouse at the very far end. You'll find us in there.'

Chief Rabat didn't say anything for a few seconds while he processed the information. Then he asked, 'How have you managed this, Mrs Fisher? You have only been in Malta for a day.'

I smiled at my end of the phone though it was a grim smile, laced with thoughts of vengeance and retribution. 'Someone chose to motivate me. Apparently, that's all it takes.'

'The Western docks,' he repeated. I'll be there as soon as I can.' Then he was gone, and I put my phone away.

'Now we wait?' asked Schneider.

'Now we tell Agent Manso Vardalos to move. But yes, now we wait,' I confirmed.

The Trap

It took about forty minutes for the Algerians to arrive. Just long enough for my bottom to get numb sitting on a pallet of sugar. We heard them arrive, but Baker was watching the approach so reported their arrival before we heard them.

My nerves were through the roof. I'm sure everyone's were so none of us talked about it. It was too late to chicken out anyway; the chess pieces were in position, all I had to do was spring the trap.

We had our captive Algerians on the ground and attached to pallets of dense sugar we could use for cover. They were in front, still zip-tied around their ankles and wrists and going nowhere. We were behind the sugar already. They weren't making any noise, at least nothing intelligible because we had gagged them. It was vital they couldn't say anything to the men coming through the door now.

The warehouse had many, many doors. One whole side was all roller doors that ascended into the ceiling, but all exits were locked except the one we left open for them. It demonstrated their confidence when they walked in without feeling the need to check what was going on inside first. They carried assault rifles or machine guns. The security team members could probably tell me exactly what make and model they were but for me it was semantics; they were brutal machines of death, that was all I needed to know.

Just behind the first half dozen gun-toting Algerians came the boss. It was obvious who he was from the room the others gave him. He wore a sharp suit in contrast to the men with guns, who were in jeans, t-shirts and sneakers. His suit was accented by a gold fob watch going into his waistcoat pocket and a sheepskin coat hung off his shoulders. He was a walking gangster cliché though I couldn't make much comment in my Sam Spade outfit. I had ditched the wig and hat at least.

Another two dozen armed men fanned out behind him. 'I seem to have you outnumbered,' the boss man observed calmly. 'Not to mention heavily outgunned. I think you should surrender.'

My knees were shaking, terrified that they might start shooting. I needed a little more time; we weren't ready yet. 'I just want the captain back,' I managed to stammer through my dry mouth.

'Ah, yes.' The boss man calmly took out a cigarette and lit it as one of his men brought him a fold out chair to sit on. He waved the match to douse it and inhaled deeply. Only once he blew a few smoke rings did he bother to answer me. 'The man we took from your hotel room. In a few moments I will tell my men to open fire. They will kill all of you. It seems the simplest way to end your annoying interference. It's nothing personal; your meddling has barely dented my evening's activities. It's the look of it, you see. Trafficking of young women is both lucrative and easy provided one makes sure the local authorities are sufficiently well paid, but I have to maintain a level of fear, leave a few bodies about every now and then.' On the ground in front of us the bound and gagged Algerian men started to shout through their gags. No one could understand the words, but the meaning was obvious. 'We might accidentally shoot them, but they shouldn't have allowed you to take them hostage. If they get caught in the crossfire, so be it.' He raised a hand.

Chief Rabat chose that moment to step out from his hiding place. I risked a smile at the surprised look on the boss man's face. All around where my team and I stood, armed police officers emerged from the shadows or from the hiding places behind boxes.

'They got here a short while before you,' I told the boss man. 'I figured you would be good enough to incriminate yourself, so I made sure the police were here to listen. You think you own the police and I counted on that, knowing you would call your tame contacts before you came here. That's why I called the chief myself, just to make sure the message got through.' I managed to sound triumphant, though at that precise moment I was standing at the centre of a wide circle of men pointing their guns at each other. If the shooting started, we would need to get somewhere else very quickly.

Chief Rabat walked forward, his men vastly outnumbering those of the Algerian he faced. The criminals' weapons tracked his progress, but he kept going, walking right up to the boss man who stood up to face the police chief as he got within a few feet.

Then they shook hands.

'Patty?' whispered Barbie. Questioning what was happening.

'So you're the man they are paying off.' I said it as a statement.

Chief Rabat turned to face me. 'Mrs Fisher, I don't know what motivated you to come here and try to mess with our trafficking operation, but I knew from your reputation that we needed to take steps against you. I thought it would be easy enough to kill you and your friend, the captain. I had him snatched so he could be killed in a dark alley. You would have been found with the murder weapon which you had then turned on yourself. You killed Fatah and Kamel in your room though which changed things and I have been trying to capture you ever since. Then you called me and wanted to set up this trap. Well,' he laughed, 'I just had to play along.'

As one, all the police weapons turned to face me and my friends.

I gulped. We were down to the wire. Then my phone beeped in my pocket and I tried desperately not to react to it. I already knew what it said. Or believed I did. I was ready for my final roll of the dice.

The Unexpected Element

With seconds left before they decided they were bored and wanted to start shooting, I spotted movement. It wasn't by the door, it was up on the roof, a shadow no one else noticed and I feared I knew what it meant. Then my fear was all but confirmed when I saw another shadow moving along the far wall way back behind the Algerians.

I had to act now. 'I expected as much, Chief Rabat. Your story about an undercover agent inside the human trafficking operation was laughable once I thought about it. An agent who was unable to determine from where they were taking people out of Malta and couldn't even find the base of operations? You need to learn to lie better. Fortunately, you will have a long time in jail to practice such skills.'

'In jail?' Chief Rabat started laughing, nudging the Algerian boss man who split a smile. The rest of the cops and criminals joined in. 'I'm the police. I have jurisdiction here. Who is going to put me in jail?'

I said, 'Actually you don't.'

He stopped laughing for a second, wiping a tear from his right eye. 'I don't what?'

'Have jurisdiction.'

'What are you talking about?' The chief wasn't able to mask the concern that crept onto his face.

'Well, you're inside a Purple Star Cruise Lines warehouse which is on a quayside owned by Purple Star Cruise Lines. As such, it is classified as international waters and therefore the security forces of Purple Star Cruise Lines have jurisdiction here.'

He stared at me, blinked a few times and went through what I had just said. He knew I was right, though he gave his head a little shake as if to clear it.

'Is that right?' asked the boss man.

Chief Rabat blinked and shook his head, glanced at his partner in crime and then turned his eyes to look at me once more. Behind him another shadow shifted, someone was getting into position. 'What does it matter?' the senior police officer asked. 'So her security guys are the ones with authority here? So what? There are six of them plus two old ladies.'

'Hey,' snapped Lady Mary.

'And there are fifty of us,' continued the chief, ignoring my friend. 'It's simple math, Mrs Fisher. You don't have enough people to win with.'

'Now,' I said calmly.

'Now?' Chief Rabat looked at the Algerian boss man to see if he understood my comment. Getting nothing, he looked back at me. 'What now? Shoot you now? I think we can arrange that.'

'Now,' I said again, a little louder this time.

Thankfully this time they reacted. A row of boxes back from where the police had taken up their hiding places, was another row of hidden figures. It hadn't been easy, this part of the trap. The more I had thought about it, the more I suspected Chief Rabat to be involved. It linked the parts and explained his behaviour. That was why I requested Commander Yusef provide some additional security which would be hidden inside the warehouse before even we arrived. They had been hunkered down out of view for most of two hours now, but on my codeword, they all stood up as one.

There were hundreds of them. More than a thousand maybe and they were all armed. It wasn't just members of the security team; there were stewards, and cleaners and chefs, plus medics, engineers and anyone and everyone that wanted to volunteer. All of them still in their uniform and all were here to ensure the rescue of their captain. We had achieved a tactical stalemate; no one was shooting.

The Algerian criminals were completely surrounded, and the police were not only complicit in their crimes but now on soil on which their badges meant nothing. Here, they were just more criminals with guns. If the Aurelia crew killed them all there would be questions, but I thought it doubtful any of them would go to jail.

I wasn't done with the hammer blows yet though. Showing the same calm demeanour the Algerian boss man had earlier, I took out my phone and opened the message. 'When you heard my phone beep a moment ago, that was from Interpol.' I saw Chief Rabat repeat the word silently. 'While you are all here, they were raiding your place on the waterfront. Quite clever hiding it inside the Virtu passenger ferry terminal. Always people and ships coming and going. All your men are in custody and Captain Alistair Huntley is on his way back here as I speak.' I raised my voice for the last few words, making sure the Aurelia's crew could hear me. My announcement got a cheer.

Then, I slipped my phone back into my pocket and fixed Chief Rabat and the Algerian with a hard stare. 'What was it you said earlier? Oh, yes. I think it's time you surrendered.'

I was able to enjoy a very, very brief moment of triumph and then the lights went out.

Someone had cut the power and it wasn't any of the police or Algerians because they were all accounted for. No, it was the spies. The ones I had seen getting ready to come through the roof which I now heard smashing above us just before the sound of glass hitting the floor reached my ears.

Then, as I knew it would, all hell broke loose. I yanked Lady Mary's arm and smacked into Barbie. The air was full of bullets and we needed to get low and get somewhere else very fast. I knocked Barbie to the floor and heard her collide with the concrete in the dark, the air whooshing out of her in one go. 'Let's go!' I yelled.

There had always been a backup plan in my head. Not that I expected the spies to find me here and come for the device twelve hours early, but we made provision for some just-in-case-this-happens kind of stuff and so had a bag stowed just behind us. I snagged it, finding Baker and the others were going for it as well. A pair of night vision goggles were thrust into my hands and the world swam into eerie green focus a second later. The others had theirs too, plus additional weapons, all of it liberated from Emily's car just in case we might need it.

Our only plan was escape. The warehouse was a bit like an amphitheatre with the bit we were standing in as the stage. Around us, in a wide semicircle, pallets were stacked upon pallets to create the tiered walls of the seating looking down onto the stage. Another word for it might be kill zone, because the Algerians and the police were stuck in the low ground, giving away every advantage. They were shooting back, but they were shooting blind and the Aurelia's crew were wise enough to stay hunkered down to shoot from defensive positions.

We ran in a straight line between the pallets, heading for the opposite side of the warehouse. We didn't slow our pace until we got there, but I knew we were safe after the first five yards; there were too many pallets full of goods for the police or Algerian bullets to reach us.

Outside and out of breath, Lady Mary clawed her goggles off. 'I think,' she panted, 'that I may have had enough excitement for one trip, Patricia,'

I patted her arm, feeling the exact same sentiment. 'Don't worry. I think it is most likely gin o'clock now.'

'Oh, thank goodness.' She sat down on a handy bollard to catch her breath. Around us, Baker, Bhukari and the others were still keeping their weapons ready, but no further threat had presented itself and the shooting had stopped inside.

Schneider said, 'We need to go back in.'

Reluctantly, I agreed. So we trudged back in, all putting our night vision goggles back on so we could see and then ripping them off again a second later, half blinded, when the lights came back on.

We found our way back to the front of the warehouse where we had been standing before. It looked different now.

'I don't want to see this,' said Lady Mary.

'Me neither,' agreed Barbie, taking her outside with Hideki holding her hand.

I didn't want to see it either. Some of the police had surrendered, as had some of the Algerians, but a lot had known they were heading straight to jail so fought it out. It hadn't gone well for them.

Commander Yusef caught my attention. 'Are you alright, Mrs Fisher?' I nodded glumly. We had won but it wasn't the sort of victory I ever wanted to be involved it. 'There are some unidentified people among the dead. I wondered if you might know anything about that?'

I sighed and said, 'Show me.' The first was only a few yards away. He was Chinese and wearing a full black tactical outfit with an expensive looking array of weapons strapped to his body. The next was toward the back of the warehouse and had a knife in his back.

'I think this one was stabbed by this one,' said Commander Yusef, pointing to another lying just around the corner. He had been garrotted. They were dressed similarly to the Chinese fellow but the first was European, possibly German and the second looked Italian.

There were seven more.

'Any idea?' asked Commander Yusef again.

'None at all,' I lied. In their determination to get to the device I held, they had killed their opposition, one wiping out the other and then being killed by the next until the last of them got shot in the hail of gun fire. I could relax if I knew this was all of them. But I didn't. I had no idea how many were left or how many might yet be deployed to get the weapon. I had to guess they were clever enough to have been watching me, they all seemed to know where I was or where I was going, all of them choosing to get to me quickly because I threatened to hand it over tomorrow morning.

To move on, I asked, 'Are there casualties on our side?' I feared the answer.

He put a reassuring hand on my shoulder. 'Nothing life threatening. Those with injuries will have something to brag about for some time to come. Purple Star Lines has a medal for acts of bravery, you know. I think they expect to hand them out for rescuing a passenger overboard rather than charging a man with a machine gun, but I think there will be quite a few being awarded after tonight. I would give one to every member of crew here if I could.'

The news that no one from the crew had been killed was the best news I could have received, but it was topped a moment later when Alistair walked through the door. Someone in the crew spotted him, I don't know who it was, but clapping started. More hands quickly joined in as they applauded the return of a man they all knew and respected and looked up to. I had acknowledged it before, but he was quite the man.

When finally his calls for calm caused the applause to die down, he said, 'I thank you, but it is I who should be applauding you. Tonight, as I understand it, the crew of the Aurelia did something no other Purple Star crew has ever done. You shot the hell out of our fresh provisions.' He let his statement hang for a moment and then the laughter started. As it grew, he had to shout to be heard. 'You are all amazing. You have done me proud, but more than that, you have done yourselves proud.' He went on for a little while longer. Praising them for their bravery, their teamwork and so on. In many ways it drove home that not only could I never take him away from this, but that I would always run second place to it. He was a lovely man. I could fall in love with him very easily if I tried. It was the wrong thing to do though and I knew it for absolute certain.

He would get to me in a moment and then apologise profusely for having to put his crew first. Some of them were injured so he was right to do so, but I drifted outside before he could. That was when I saw a man I already loved.

'Madam, I appear to have missed something. Are you alright?'

A tear fell from my eye and I got that pain you feel in the back of your throat when you are so sad or so emotional that you just cannot control it. I hugged him tightly to me. Between sobs, I managed, 'When did you get out?'

'Almost an hour ago, madam. The lawyer, Mr O'Donnell, was very apologetic that it took this long. I went back to the ship to find you but learned you were here attempting to rescue the captain. I trust everything went according to whatever plan you devised.'

'Close enough, Jermaine. Close enough.'

Lady Mary spotted me, 'Come along, Patricia dear, I'm parched. Can we get back to the ship now?'

'Ah,' said Jermaine, unhooking a small backpack. 'I took the precaution of bringing provisions.'

Outside the warehouse, using the top of a concrete bollard as a table, Jermaine produced a battery powered chiller from his backpack, an ice bucket with ice and silver tongs, plus a cloth to polish them, several cans of Fevertree slimline tonic and two bottles of Hendricks gin. My eyes lit up like a fruit machine paying out the jackpot. Lady Mary almost fainted with joy.

The clean up would take hours, Interpol would coordinate everything and want statements, but I no longer cared. I had Jermaine back, my friends were safe, and I had a cold glass of gin to enjoy.

Alistair found the nine of us halfway through our second glass, all sitting on the floor in the warm evening air as we waited for the operation to reach a point where it was acceptable for us to leave. Two gins was definitely borderline too much for me to drive after, so it was a good thing we didn't have far to go and we would be in and around the docks the whole time. In the morning the rental Toyotas could be returned; no one was doing it now, but I had elected to abandon Emily's Alfa Romeo. I thought about keeping it, but it wasn't mine and I had no way of knowing if the organisation that did own it might have a tracking device hidden somewhere. The security team would deal with the weapons and things.

Alistair bent down to give me a hug and I returned it warmly, letting him pull me to my feet so we could step away to talk in private.

'I'm sorry I couldn't come to you first, darling. I...'

I put a finger to his lips. 'It's okay, Alistair. You have a ship to captain and a crew who love you.'

He nodded, relieved that I understood. 'We didn't get to spend much time together after all, despite our plans, did we?'

'No. No, we didn't,' I agreed.

'For the first time ever, I shall be glad to leave Malta. It is no longer a favourite place. I think, in fact, that I shall see if I can arrange the cruises to not stop here for a few years. There are so many other places in the Mediterranean after all.'

'There certainly are,' I agreed again, silently noting that he would be going around and around the planet for years to come.

He started to walk me back to my friends. 'I will make sure there is a car to get you back to the ship shortly. Perhaps tomorrow we can have breakfast together?'

'It will need to be dinner instead. I still have an errand to run tomorrow.'

His brow knitted in confusion. 'An errand?'

The Maltese Parrot

Barbie came with me to distract herself. Lady Mary came with me because she hadn't seen Malta, she said. I think the real reason was that she wanted to see the conclusion to the story.

Hideki left the ship at six o'clock this morning. He had to catch a flight to London's Heathrow Airport and then from there a long-haul overnight flight to Tokyo. That was why Barbie needed to be distracted. It wasn't working though.

'What if I never see him again?' she asked, the question directed at herself rather than to me or Lady Mary. She had Anna on her lap because I put her there, another distraction tactic I employed because it gave Barbie something to do with her hands. My dog would give her a little grumpy whining noise if Barbie stopped stroking or fussing her for more than a few seconds.

'You can see him if you want to,' I pointed out.

'But what if he gets a hospital in Japan? A hospital anywhere in the states would do. I could move there and get a job and we could try. I'm not sure I could move to Japan. I know it's a double standard because he will move to my country, but I don't want to reciprocate...'

'It's okay,' I cut in before she could say the same thing again. 'At this point in time he could go anywhere, right? And he applied to more American hospitals than anywhere else, right? Wait until you know. Then deal with what comes of it. Torturing yourself now does you no good.' It was about the fifth time I had said the same thing.

'You're right, Patty,' she acknowledged, wiping away a tear.

Lady Mary forced a welcome change of subject. 'Is it much farther?'

'About ten more minutes,' said the driver.

'What did you tell them?' asked Barbie.

The 'them' she referred to was the Tanners; the irksome family with the missing grandmother. It was getting close to midnight when I got back to the ship the previous evening, my journey there conducted on the edge of my seat as I wondered if there were any more government agents about to jump out on me. With all that had gone on and despite all the people who had died, I still had the stupid data device with the weapon on it in my bag.

I almost went to the gate of Valetta for nine o'clock this morning but decided I just couldn't be bothered. I hadn't seen Justin in over twenty-four hours so perhaps he had been killed too. I was stuck with it, but I had already decided on a course of action to resolve that. Instead of going to Valetta's ancient entry gate, I phoned James Barnstable again, and this time, rather than ask him any questions, I gave him instructions instead.

My instructions were clear and specific and came with a threat. He elected to acquiesce, which was why, less than ten minutes later, our driver pulled into a restaurant overlooking the waterfront in St Paul's Bay.

The driver opened my door and offered his hand to help me out. Anna plopped out first, plop being the right word for her as she seemed to have gained more girth in the few hours we had been apart. Possibly the bridge crew members had overfed her, unable to resist her Oscar-worthy hungry look.

'What are we doing here?' asked Sarah Tanner.

'Meeting your mother,' I replied. 'Exactly as I told you before we left.'

'But I don't understand. What is she doing here? Was she taken or not?'

I didn't reply. Gary Senior was still shouting at his son to put his phone down and get out of the car. He showed no sign of winning. I left them to it and led the way inside the building where a waiter indicated that we were expected and directed us to a terrace at the back. Before I got there, a grey-haired man blocked my path.

'James Barnstable?' I asked, certain I had it right. He looked like his picture from Nora Garland's wedding day. Or rather, he looked like the grandfather of the man in the picture.

It was him. 'Yes. You're Patricia Fisher then. Nora's not happy. She thought she had escaped, you see?'

'I'm sure.'

'Who's this?' asked Sarah. She had given up on her husband and kids and followed me inside.

Over at the bar, Lady Mary was instructing the barman on how to mix the perfect gin cocktail for an ailing heart and prescribing one to Barbie.

I fixed James with an apologetic look. 'I think you should show her.'

He nodded. Unhappy, but aware that he had little choice. It was the right thing to do.

As Sarah followed him out of the door and onto the terrace, I heard her cry of shock, then the door swung shut and cut off most of what was then said. I was glad. I didn't need to hear it.

'Pour me one.' I took a seat at the bar so that Lady Mary and I sat either side of the sad girl - an emotional support sandwich. My drink arrived a moment later, and I sniffed it, staring over the top of the glass at the stuffed parrot behind the bar.

No one knew what James had admitted to me when I called him for the second time this morning. He and Nora met in this bar fifty-three years ago. She arrived after taking an exciting job with the Navy Army Air Force Institute, otherwise known as the NAAFI. They supplied staff to bars and clubs in British forces barracks and bases around the world. Her first assignment had been Malta and at the time, the bar had been the off-base place her husband's squadron all went to. It had been for years, which was how the unit got the parrot nickname.

Nora and James enjoyed a brief fling as a couple, but he was sent away, the Navy moving personnel about continuously then as they still do now. They both thought that was that, but he came back six months later, the post he had gone to getting closed. By then she had met and accepted the hand of the man she went on to marry, only to find out that he and James were best friends. They stayed in contact all these years and now that both their spouses had passed on, they acknowledged a flame that had never gone out.

Nora wasn't planning to go home. Quite what her daughter might make of that I couldn't tell, but it was none of my business. Gary, Gary, and the super silent daughter whose name I couldn't remember, all followed Sarah out on to the terrace.

I finished my gin, nudged Barbie, and the three of us went back to our car. The Tanners had a couple of hours to work things out and get back to the ship. Or not. It was their choice entirely.

I slept on my way back to the ship, the events of the last two days catching up with me. Anna slept too, snoring all the way back to the ship.

Safely back on board, I looked forward to moving on. Malta had not been what I expected, but then neither had Athens, or Zangrabar for that matter. Thinking about it, more than half the places I visited, resulted in some kind of drama. Perhaps I should throw my passport away when I get home. I smiled to myself at my idle musings and let Anna pull me into my suite. Barbie wanted to blow off some cobwebs with a good workout, so I was going to join her. As usual, I really didn't feel like it, which was how I knew I needed to do it.

Anna trotted across to the kitchen to see what Jermaine was up to. I gave him a wave in reply to his salutation and went to my bedroom to change.

I closed the door and kicked off my shoes, then clamped my hand over my mouth so I wouldn't scream.

Stupid Mass Storage Device

'Hello, Mrs Fisher,' said Justin Metcalf-Howe. 'My apologies for making you jump again.'

I used the wall for support and let my hand fall away. 'How did you get in here without my butler seeing you?'

He frowned at the question. 'It's my job, Mrs Fisher. I'm supposed to get into places without being seen.'

I didn't bother to pursue it any further. 'Have you come for the device?'

'I have,' he said happily. 'I assume it is still in your possession.' I reached into my handbag and threw it to him. He caught it one handed, his hand flashing out to snatch it from the air. 'Thank you.'

'No, thank you. Thank you for the danger, murder, explosions, kidnappings, threat, blood, and general terror of the last two days.' I was being flippant, and he knew it.

'Your country owes you a great debt of gratitude.'

'Yeah, yeah, you told me that already. Why don't you tell me what that thing does?' I had been carrying it around and protecting it like it was a baby for two days and I wanted to know why.

He pursed his lips and stared into the middle distance for a moment while he ran an internal debate. Reaching a decision, he shrugged. 'It attacks a nation's computer systems. Now that so much is controlled by computers, it is possible to shut down electricity, gas, and water. Ground all aircraft, turn off all the traffic lights, wipe out a stock exchange. The list goes on. It can be remotely controlled from a single computer located anywhere on the planet, so the attacker doesn't even need to be in the country they are attacking. They just need an operative to get the device into a computer fitted with the hardware to handle it and they can use the internet to conduct a cyber-attack that would make the nuclear bomb feel like a bad hangover. It's actually very clever.'

I guess I understood now why everyone wanted it. 'It's yours now. I won't see you again, will I?' I made it clear with my voice that it was my preferred option.

'No, Mrs Fisher,' he said, getting up and tucking the device into his jacket. At the door, he paused and turned. 'Goodbye, Mrs Fisher. Good luck.'

Then he was gone. I listened to see if there would be an altercation when Jermaine saw him, or if Anna would go nuts, but neither thing happened. Curious, I popped my head back out of my bedroom door. There was no sign of Justin, Anna was asleep on the couch, and Jermaine was in the kitchen playing chef as he whipped up something tasty for my lunch.

I checked out the sun terrace, looking along the length of the ship, forward and aft but there was no sign of him. I had no idea how Justin did it, but I was glad he was on our side. Then I thought about that. What did I actually know about Justin? He claimed to be British Intelligence, but it wasn't like spies carried ID, so I had taken his word on faith. I couldn't even tell if the name he gave me was real.

Considering that, and then remembering Emily's wonderful Kensington accent, I decided it was probably a good thing I gave him the dummy device. The familiar rumble of the Aurelia's giant engines reached my ears as they started up for the series of checks they needed to perform before we put to sea. We would be moving within the hour, but we didn't need to be out to sea to do what I needed to do. I unzipped the part of my handbag the real device was in and dropped it over the side. It vanished from sight before it made it to the water. The computer boffins that made it were dead, and now so was their horrific invention.

Heading back to my bedroom, I decided Barbie was right; I needed to blow out some cobwebs as well. A good workout would settle me.

My phone rang just as I was tying my shoelaces. I expected it to be Barbie to say she was there already or to say she got tied up and was running late, but it was neither.

The name on my caller display was Charlie, my soon-to-be ex-husband. I stared at it for a few seconds, the phone continuing to ring and vibrate in my hand. Managing to snap myself out of the surprise I felt, I swiped the button to answer the call.

'Charlie?'

'Patricia, I need your help.'

I almost scoffed at him, but something about his tone stopped me from doing so. 'What is it, Charlie. What's wrong?'

'It's Maggie,' he said, pausing before he continued which gave me enough time to feel my rage rising. He was having relationship problems with the woman with whom he cheated on me, and he dared to come to me for advice. 'It's Maggie,' he repeated. 'She's been murdered.'

The End

Author note:

It is a little after ten o'clock on a Monday morning. I finished writing this just before two this morning but couldn't find the effort then to write my little author note. Instead, I stole about three and a half hours sleep before my over-excited four-year-old mammoth child arrived with a host of demands which included playing Hungry Hippos and breakfast, though not necessarily in that order.

I chose Malta for the setting this time because I have been there many times myself. My wife and I even considered buying a place before our nocturnal activities resulted in the before-mentioned mammoth child. Malta is a short hop for us, living as we do, in the south of England. Breakfast flights have seen us in the pool and feeling very much on holiday before noon on more than one occasion. Not a bad change of pace having finished work the previous evening.

Oddly, now that I write for a living and don't consider it to really be work because I enjoy it so much, I don't have weekends or holidays. As the calendar approaches Christmas, there will be no office party, nor a break from work that, in the past, I have always been yearning for. This is not a bad thing. Just a new thing.

I have one more book in this series to write and have already started it. If you fear for the end of Patricia's tale, worry not, for there will be more to come. There will be other series with entirely new characters too as I stretch my legs, pray I don't get cramp in my fingers, and keep on churning out the words.

I have a milestone birthday next year; one I am quite happy to meet head on though I often find myself listening to people moan about getting older. I consider it vastly more appealing than the alternative. There are other events next year which will dominate though, my milestone fading into insignificance by comparison. I'll happily tell you all about them later.

Or you can choose to follow me more closely by signing up to my newsletter. You can find links to it at my website if that appeals.

https://stevehiggsbooks.com/

Patricia's adventures are not my first series though; there are many other books already waiting for you. So, if you enjoy Patricia's adventures, you may wish to check out **Tempest Michaels**, **Amanda Harper** and **Jane Butterworth**. Like Patricia, they solve mysteries and their stories are written to make you laugh and keep you turning pages when you really ought to be going to sleep.

Finally, there is a **Patricia Fisher** story that you may not yet have found. It is part of this series but sits apart from it. It is called **Killer Cocktail** and you can have it for free. Just click the link below and tell me where to send it.

Yes! Send me my FREE Patricia Fisher story!

The Missing Sapphire of Zangrabar
The Kidnapped Bride
The Director's Cut

The Couple in Cabin 2124
Doctor Death
Murder on the Dancefloor
Mission for the Maharaja
A Sleuth and her Dachshund in Athens
The Maltese Parrot
No Place Like Home

Printed in Great Britain
by Amazon